# THE
# LEV
# EFFECT

*A Novel*

Sheldon Greene

The Lev Effect

Sheldon Greene/KinurPub Publishing
www.sheldongreene.com/

Publisher's Note: This is a work of fiction. Names, characters, places, and incidents are a product of the author's imagination. Locales and public names are sometimes used for atmospheric purposes. Any re- semblance to actual people, living or dead, or to businesses, companies, events, institutions, or locales is completely coincidental.

ISBN: 979-8-999454953-1-0 (paperback)
ISBN: 979-8-9865505-6-5 (eBook)

Book Interior & E-book Design: Amit Dey (amitdey2528@gmail.com)

# Other novels by Sheldon Greene

Lost and Found

Burnt Umber

Prodigal Sons

Pursuit of Happiness

The Seed Apple

The Lev Effect

Tamar

# Table of Contents

Preface . . . . . . . . . . . . . . . . . . . . . . . . . . . . . . . . . . . . . . . . . . . . vii

1. Words . . . . . . . . . . . . . . . . . . . . . . . . . . . . . . . . . . . . . . . . . . 1

2. Courage. . . . . . . . . . . . . . . . . . . . . . . . . . . . . . . . . . . . . . . . . 7

3. The Talk of Elders . . . . . . . . . . . . . . . . . . . . . . . . . . . . . . . . 13

4. A Faithful Friend. . . . . . . . . . . . . . . . . . . . . . . . . . . . . . . . . 21

5. Red Star in the East. . . . . . . . . . . . . . . . . . . . . . . . . . . . . . . 29

6. The Kettle and the Crock . . . . . . . . . . . . . . . . . . . . . . . . . . 33

7. Guide to the Perplexed . . . . . . . . . . . . . . . . . . . . . . . . . . . 41

8. Calling the Lost Sheep. . . . . . . . . . . . . . . . . . . . . . . . . . . . 47

9. Daily Bread . . . . . . . . . . . . . . . . . . . . . . . . . . . . . . . . . . . . 55

10. On Forgiving Debts . . . . . . . . . . . . . . . . . . . . . . . . . . . . . 61

11. Equal Treatment . . . . . . . . . . . . . . . . . . . . . . . . . . . . . . . . 65

12. What a Candle Knows. . . . . . . . . . . . . . . . . . . . . . . . . . . . 77

13. Swallow A Cow . . . . . . . . . . . . . . . . . . . . . . . . . . . . . . . . . 81

14. What to Do With The Right Eye . . . . . . . . . . . . . . . . . . . 87

15. Light in The Darkness. . . . . . . . . . . . . . . . . . . . . . . . . . . . 95

16. Portents. . . . . . . . . . . . . . . . . . . . . . . . . . . . . . . . . . . . . . 103

17. Pseudepigrapha . . . . . . . . . . . . . . . . . . . . . . . . . . . . . . . 109

18. Old Friends . . . . . . . . . . . . . . . . . . . . . . . . . . . . . . . . . . . 115

19. Going Fishing . . . . . . . . . . . . . . . . . . . . . . . . . . . . . . . . . . 121

20. Not Even A Pillow. . . . . . . . . . . . . . . . . . . . . . . . . . . . . . . 133

21. Looking For Signs . . . . . . . . . . . . . . . . . . . . . . . . . . . . . . . 139

22. Edible Flowers. . . . . . . . . . . . . . . . . . . . . . . . . . . . . . . . . . 147

23. A Close Shave . . . . . . . . . . . . . . . . . . . . . . . . . . . . . . . . . . 159

24. Heart's Counsel . . . . . . . . . . . . . . . . . . . . . . . . . . . . . . . . . 163

25. Late Love Early . . . . . . . . . . . . . . . . . . . . . . . . . . . . . . . . . 167

26. Knowing the Trees. . . . . . . . . . . . . . . . . . . . . . . . . . . . . . . 175

27. False Witness. . . . . . . . . . . . . . . . . . . . . . . . . . . . . . . . . . . 183

28. The Price of Sparrows . . . . . . . . . . . . . . . . . . . . . . . . . . . . 191

29. The Sheep Fold . . . . . . . . . . . . . . . . . . . . . . . . . . . . . . . . . 195

30. At Supper . . . . . . . . . . . . . . . . . . . . . . . . . . . . . . . . . . . . . 201

31. Reprieve . . . . . . . . . . . . . . . . . . . . . . . . . . . . . . . . . . . . . . 205

32. Overcoming the World . . . . . . . . . . . . . . . . . . . . . . . . . . . 213

33. Credo . . . . . . . . . . . . . . . . . . . . . . . . . . . . . . . . . . . . . . . . 217

34. By Man Came Also . . . . . . . . . . . . . . . . . . . . . . . . . . . . . . 223

35. Hallelujah . . . . . . . . . . . . . . . . . . . . . . . . . . . . . . . . . . . . . 229

36. Life Insurance . . . . . . . . . . . . . . . . . . . . . . . . . . . . . . . . . . 235

37. A Song of Songs . . . . . . . . . . . . . . . . . . . . . . . . . . . . . . . . 239

Epilogue. . . . . . . . . . . . . . . . . . . . . . . . . . . . . . . . . . . . . . . . . 243

# Preface

## by the author
## An introduction to the
## American Quartet

The American Quartet is comprised of four of my novels, Lost and Found, The Seed Apple, The Lev Effect and Tamar. Mendel Traig is the common narrator of the first three and appears in the epilogue of Tamar. The first three are sequels. Lost and Found and The Lev Effect take place in Bolton PA with overlapping characters. Tamar is narrated by the chief character and is the prequel of the Seed Apple. Tamar and the Seed Apple take place in the Southern California desert.

The first book in the quartet, narrated by Mendel Traig, *Lost and Found*, published by Random House is set in the fifties after WW II in an imaginary small town, Bolton Pa.

In **Lost and Found,** Mendel, a Holocaust survivor chooses between life in Bolton and reparations in Israel. "Gentle, funny, poignant, and magical the book celebrates the small miracles of ordinary life." A rabbi discovers he can heal. Sterile people give birth. A mysterious bookstore burns.

A cookbook divides the sisterhood. Refugees are welcomed. The Los Angeles Times Book Review gave it a **Critics Commendation** and said, "**Greene is a born storyteller**" The Indianapolis News wrote, "...**The book goes down like fine vintage wine. Lost & Found is a beautiful work beautifully done...**" ; "immensely entertaining"; Dallas Morning News; "universal truths of fabulous implication"; Cleveland Plain Dealer. "It belongs on the same bookshelf with Mark Twain." Hadassah Magazine

In **The Seed Apple**, Mendel travels to the California desert and engages a family of Jewish Native Americans who trace their origin to Pre-Hispanic Yucatan. Focusing on the Binyan's, a family of builders, was a natural extension of the concept of Solomon's sailors having a cross-cultural impact on the Mayans. It's also a re-telling of the Exodus story. The Cold War setting supported the construction of the latest tower on their Sacred Mountain, which is designed to communicate globally with our nuclear submarine fleet. This provided an opportunity to express the inter-generational tensions that were an intrinsic element of that period. An additional theme is the emergence of strong women, breaking out of their traditional roles. This was incidentally a major theme in an earlier novel, *Burnt Umber.*

The archaeological evidence that was the idea for the novel suggests an early Christian influence on the Mayan civilization. Specifically, there is a sculptural bas relief, known as the Cross Temple of Palenque. It depicts a cruciform as its central theme. Seeing this sparked my imagination. There were myths dealing with Solomon's maritime fleet, evidence of early Norse exploration of North America, before Columbus, and tales of

Christian Missionaries crossing the Atlantic. History is after all a torn cloth. Where do mythology and archeology intersect?

The third novel, **The Lev Effect** , returns to Bolton and is a re-telling of the Passion. This one is also narrated by Mendel Traig. The Bolton PA. Jewish Community converts a disused old people's home into a boarding school and hires a Russian refugee to run it and the retirees to staff it. The old residents love the change, but things get dicey when the director admits a Palestinian boy, schedules Palestine National Day and a dinner fund raiser for a Catholic homeless shelter. The family that endowed the place 50 years ago sues to get their trust fund back. A teenage hacker manages to find alternative funding by manipulating resident's pension accounts. An enemy on the faculty tries to get the director deported. When the director dies some people think that he was Jesus. The Lev Effect is full of warmth, humor and the celebration of the extraordinary in the ordinary which should appeal to the faithful of all religions and iconoclasts alike.

"The author's artful brew of farcical comedy and theological provocation may remind readers of the work of Booker Prize–winning novelist Howard Jacobson. Overall, it's a delightfully satirical exploration of the intersection between the quotidian and the absurd. Lev is a particularly memorable character; it turns out that when he said "superintendent," he actually meant "janitor," and he neither encourages nor repudiates the strange notion that his arrival is the fulfillment of biblical prophecy. Throughout, Greene wisely explores the salutary power of faith, which Mendel calls a "kind of spiritual walker for the psychologically disabled. A profoundly funny meditation on how one can find strength in religion". Kirkus Review

"This story had me tearing up in analysis then soaring in joy. There's not a better time than now to encourage acceptance of differences and to search for and celebrate Goodness wherever it exists. Can we not use this tale as a guide at this time of year, to search out the best in everyone? This author's style will sing to your soul. I strongly recommend you read this, absorbing its hauntingly beautiful melody in its message." Book Review Crew

"In his warm-hearted novel Sheldon Greene touches on life's deepest questions via a community of characters committed to a Jewish retirement home cum boarding school. Humor, clear plotting, fine character portrayals, and vivid—even poetic—descriptions of the sensory world carry the throb of life. After reading the book, I sat with the same thought one of the characters articulates: "Once again I saw the good and I was glad" Susan Phillips , Exec Director , New College, Graduate Theological Union, U.C. Berkeley

The fourth novel Tamar, is the late 19th century Binyan back story narrated by Tamar Binyan, who was the family leader. In this coming of age novel, Tamar must contend with her impulsive husband, the birth of a child, an affair, the displacement and relocation of the community, to mention some of the challenges. Tamar was awarded the silver medal for family saga fiction- Global Book Awards.

"*Tamar* ... - depicts the tumultuous journey of a Jewish/American Indian community who find themselves dispossessed of their ancestral land. The story intimately follows the leader of the community, Tamar, as she navigates such unprecedented events: the building of a railroad, settlers, war, and the relocation of her people to an industrialized world. **An inspiring,** visceral novel, *Tamar* will leave you breathless with its wholly unique perspective on this period of history. The dichotomy Greene creates between artificial America and Tamar›s community further illuminates life›s most fundamental modes of survival- self-sufficiency, community, love, and resilience - for a profoundly stirring work of historical fiction." -SelfPublishingReview.com

Creative expression finds an outlet in many ways. For me, it's the written word. I sometimes think that creative writing is an attempt to bring to fruition an alternative to reality, be it the externalization of fear or wish fulfillment. As a lawyer with a public policy track record, the motivation is the same, to be an active change agent, to make the world a better place. The writing and the law are different expressions of the same motivation, I suspect. But there is something unique about the experience of creative writing. What I find almost magical about the process is that once the characters have taken shape in my imagination, they take on a life of their own.

Enjoy!

Sheldon Greene

# ONE

# Words

Nudelman started it.

"I want Isaac to have a real education," he said, looking around at the Synagogue Board with his wise hound's eyes.

Those were the words that began it all. Just eight words; a few sounds tossed into the air of the boardroom. But words have power. They can make people kill, make them fall in love, even buy appliances they don't need.

Nobody paid attention to Nudelman that day. There were more pressing matters to be decided at that meeting, like where to get the money for re-wiring the sanctuary. The eternal light kept going out and if you can't have an eternal light over the ark, what kind of a sanctuary is it? Although some would say that the Torah has its own light, but not everybody can see it.

It's easy to find the money for a nice stained-glass window, but who wants a bronze plaque that says "Abe Strauss, circuit breaker"?

Here I am, not even a page into my story and already digressing. Sorry. You have a right to go from here to there in a reasonably direct route, not by way of Minsk and Pinsk, as my Uncle Mayer used to say. On the other hand, who knows what you'll see in Pinsk? Listen! Put this book down right now and go on to something less airy than the Messiah and his coming. No? You're curious. Good.

Nudelman didn't let it drop. He kept pushing the idea of a Jewish day school. They don't call him Needleman for nothing. He constantly complained about the public schools in Bolton, the thirty-five students to a class, the dumbing-down of the textbooks. He'd say, "There's no texture to history; it reads like a deodorant commercial," "The crime and drugs!" and "My God, school is like life!" He'd rage about the lack of amenities: "The school doesn't even have an orchestra anymore. Can you imagine a violinist in the school band marching down the football field?" He'd mention the shallowness of the kids' Jewish culture: "They care more about the Young Judea dances than the Bible." Not that Nudelman was a great, or even a trivial, biblical scholar, but maybe he saw a lack in himself and wanted more for Isaac, his only child.

His carping and harping went on for about a year, until one evening, at the end of a long meeting, Finkelstein's eyes looked ready to pop as he glared across the polished mahogany of the board of directors' table, slapped down his spiral secretary's notebook, and hollered, "What do you want from us? Stop already with the Jewish day school. It's impossible! A dream. A fantasy! You want a school? Move to Pittsburgh!"

By the look of him, Nudelman wasn't bothered by the outburst. Not at all. Nudelman had finally touched a nerve. They were listening. He hit the accelerator and peeled rubber—you could almost smell it.

"Bolton's Jewish community is going the way of Megiddo," he said. Nobody but Rabbi Bing knew what he was talking about. "If one more family moves to Phoenix, we can open an archeological park and sell tickets. We need to do something that will restore the vitality of the community. And my solution is a Jewish boarding school."

A shiver of approval, less than a nod, came from Rabbi Bing, but the rest of the Board glowered. Rosenzweig, a lawyer and no friend of private education, took the lead. He shook his head, causing his jowls to quiver like Jello, and pronounced, "You think you're the Music Man, Nudelman? Let me give not one no, but three nos. No money. No building. No students."

"Not exactly," Nudelman retorted . He drew a little circle on his scratch pad then looked at each of them in turn, his face showing the after-blush of a secret joke.

"Nudelman has had a letter from the Reparations Board," said Dr. Zucker., Phil Feld pulled a cigar out of his suit pocket. Chastened by Heda Finkelstein's frown, he contented himself with crinkling the cellophane between his fingers.

"Are you going to watch the Pirates game?" he asked Finkelstein, who looked in response as though someone had already blown smoke in his eyes.

About that time Nudelman, was standing, preparing for a dramatic exit, when Rabbi Bing, always the conciliator, stopped him with a firm touch from his long fingers.

"Let's once and for all hear Nudelman out on this, shall we?" He raised his head heavenward for emphasis, as if he expected God to vote. Then he gave one of his sweep-the-room-full-of-meaning glances from behind his inch-thick lenses. The rabbi's palm flipped and gracefully gestured toward Nudelman, who remained standing, poised over the table, as if he were preparing to vault across it. (Nudelman had vaulted for Bolton High.)

"How many Jewish boarding schools are there in this country?" Nudelman asked, and before anyone could speak, he answered, "None?"

"So what!" said Rosenzweig, leaning his bulk into the words. "You might as well ask how many crocodiles there are in the Monoganessen River. It is beyond our small means. The Pritzkers (he meant rich people) chose to make their home a bit farther down the turnpike in Chicago."

"Hear him out," said Rabbi Bing, with a sprinkle of pepper in his usually mild tone. "Don't interrupt."

"Thank you, Rabbi Bing," said Nudelman. "Don't think I haven't thought about it. Maybe this'll shock you, but when you think about it, it'll make some sense."

"Get on with it, Nudelman, life is passing you by," Finkelstein chided.

"OK."

"Do that." Finkelstein just had to have the last word.

"It's simple."

"We're all ears." Finkelstein does in fact have big ears.

"The Home for the Aged."

"So? What about it?"

Nudelman's hound eyes lit up with a vision.

"As you know, it was built as a TB sanitarium in 1912," he began, "converted in 1947 to a home for the elderly. It has spacious grounds, a solid stone Tudor gothic building, room for 150 maybe 200 if we pack them in, and an endowment, the Mossberg Trust, you all know what that's worth in income. What is it, $400,000? And thanks to aerobics, golf, vitamins, triple bypasses and Leisure World condos in the sun, we have just five—count 'em: five—seniors rattling around the place."

"So what do you have in mind? Should we sell the place and move the rest of them to Phoenix?" Rosenzweig said, shaking his leonine head. "It can't be done; we've been through that before. Close the Home for the Aged and the money goes to the Jewish Home for Parents in Pittsburgh. And they've already got enough to supply every resident with their choice of a Steinberg piano."

"Steinway!" said Heda Finkelstein, gazing up over her half-lenses from her knitting. Heda had one.

"Or a motorized wheelchair made by Cadillac," Rosenzweig muttered.

Nudelman looked like Edison when the light bulb started to glow. He rose up to his full five feet ten inches, opened both of his hands and proclaimed, "We don't have to. That's what I've concluded after reading the original trust. Rosenzweig, you'll like this: a section that says you can provide for all the needs of the residents."

"So, buy a color television, even a Jacuzzi!"

"What about things to do, companionship? The school will be like therapy. The old folks will teach the young, give them values, and give them a sense of history, of generational change. And the kids will keep them company, just like grandchildren."

"That's a novel idea," said Roe. "But as I recall only one of them was a teacher. What's her name?"

"Miss Leventhal," I said. She had been my English teacher and Nudelman's and a few of the others as well "We'll hire a staff of teachers, who will spend part of their time in a learning-in-retirement program."

"Nudelman, I've got to hand it to you, you should be Secretary of the Treasury. You could turn the deficit into a surplus," said Finkelstein, grinning around the table for confirmation.

"What do you think, Mendel?" asked Rabbi Bing. I was there to take notes, one of my duties as the Community Center Administrator—a fancy title intended to take the place of a better salary.

"Well," I began, looking around for signs of approval. No doubt about it, Nudelman had finally turned a little credibility valve in each of them. Everyone on the Board had wanted somehow to crack the stone sheath that surrounded the Old Folks Trust, as it was called. And Nudelman, they were all thinking, had possibly found the cabbalistic formula. "I like the idea," I finally said.

"You know, Nudelman. A Jewish boarding school isn't such a bad idea, now that I think of it," added Rosenzweig, pulling on a left jowl with his frankfurter-sized fingers and looking around at the others,

And so, I learned something else about the gears and machinations of human events. Ideas germinate for a long time before they find validation in others. Look at Galileo, Columbus, Spinoza and the tough time they all had selling their concepts. It's not the idea itself but the way it's packaged that matters most, it seems. And whether it gives someone something they might like but don't have, that matters most of all. Now don't just get the idea that Nudelman had carried off a *fait accompli*, not by a long shot. But his bat had hit the ball and he was running like hell toward first base.

# TWO

# Courage

Obsession is not too strong a word to describe Nudelman's dedication to the Jewish boarding school. Seeing him badger and cajole made me think of the energy he and Sarah had concentrated on the problem of having a child. Years had passed but they never stopped trying and finally it happened. Now here he was again, swimming against the current like a spawning salmon Isaac, their son, was now thirteen, all elbows and knees, self-conscious with a breaking voice and a few pimples—a young Nudelman with the same thick black hair and large expressive brown eyes.

One of our high school buddies once said, "Nudelman sees with his ears and hears with his eyes." He played guard on the Bolton High basketball team and I remember how fast he was. In fact, Nudelman was Most Valuable Player his senior year even though Bolton lost the divisional to Slippery Rock. About nine years back, he had sold the family plumbing supply business to a large Pittsburgh chain for what most people said was a killing, although everybody always says that about the other guy. After a few months of looking around, including three weeks on Nassau, he had the guts to buy the local GM truck dealership after the 86-year-old owner, Walter C. Taffey, broke his hip changing a tire during a teamster's strike. Everybody said he got a bargain. Rumor had it that Taffey still remembered Nudelman's winning basket the night the Bolton five stole the championship from Beaver Falls.

What did Nudelman know about trucks? Nothing, but that didn't stop him; after all, he knew how to run a business. And he made a go of it with discounts, leasing, fleet rates and who knows what else. He even installed a computer to keep track of parts, which was better than relying on Mr. Taffey's memory, so the customers said.

Every year Nudelman and Sarah did better and better. They were giving a lot more money to the synagogue and they were spending long weekends in New York seeing plays, eating in Italian restaurants that Sarah found in *Gourmet*, even buying an occasional painting and replacing the framed Matisse and Cezanne posters. Enough of that. All it shows is that Nudelman doesn't let go once he starts.

Watching Nudelman chip away at the Board made me think that there are two kinds of achievements—big and little. Most of us are content with the little: getting up on time, catching the bus. Our lives are a pile of acts, benign and banal, unique in a way but undistinguished.

Then there are the few who somehow move boulders. Looking at the boulder-movers , we who can't are left to wonder how they can. History is full of them: Madame Curie, Columbus, Hannibal, Alexander, Balzac, Shakespeare, Ben Gurion, Washington and the others, the nameless bush-league heroes, people like Nudelman. Their secret is that they don't see how impossible their goals are. They too just get up in the morning and put on their shoes, just like Nudelman. By the way, his first name was Nachman, but nobody ever called him that— nobody could pronounce it.

He didn't look much like a truck dealer the day I went up to his home office, over his two-car garage. No shoes on and a hole in his sock. His blue wool sweater was faded and the rumpled moss green corduroy pants bagged at the knees. As usual that thicket of ungovernable black hair was in need of pruning. Maybe that's why people trust Nudelman; he doesn't look like a sharpy and he's not.

The room, his study, was as rumpled as he was, piled with discarded or half-read *Wall Street Journals* and *Popular Mechanics* open to articles he wanted to get back to someday. Even with the window open there was a smell of pipe smoke and dog. Mandalay, an old Labrador retriever, grey at the muzzle and milky in the eye, lay at his feet on a faded hand-hooked circular rug. In front of him, Nudelman, not the dog, was a mosaic, with little notes on scraps of paper of different sizes and colors covering him.

"Mendel. Glad you could come." He had a sharp voice, urgent, like every sports announcer I've ever heard. He thrust his long-fingered hand toward me and asked, "Rosenzweig gave you the agreement?"

"Yes, I have it here, but don't ask me what it says. It's all commas and no periods."

"Better you don't know, and then nobody will blame you if we blow it."

"What's it all about?"

"Just a formality. A long-winded resolution, from the trustees of the old folks' home, to the effect that funds can be spent for education, recreation, and therapy for the residents at the discretion of the Board."

"So that's all it takes, Nudelman? I've got to hand it to you, you're a magician."

Nudelman raised his hand and let it fall, dismissing the accomplishment. "All I did, Mendel, was show them how to turn on the lamp."

"I have to say, though, I've been wondering what Mr. Mossberg would have said." Mossberg had set up the trust in the late twenties.

"We'll discuss it with the lawyer."

"There may be relatives who would just as soon have the money. I've heard of such things."

"They're long gone, as far as I know; don't worry about it. We've got a million things to do: recruit teachers, find a director, advertise in the Jewish papers for students, buy sporting equipment, books, desks. It's endless. I'm glad you're experienced, what with the synagogue school." As he spoke he was rearranging the little notes.

"Have you talked to the old folks about it?"

"You should do that, Mendel. You've got a way with them."

I knew he would say that. It all eventually comes to me as the amanuensis of the synagogue and factotum of the Board, not that they don't do their share. But I get paid for what I do. No matter. I like the old folks and thought, as Nudelman did, that the idea of a school in their midst would be as energizing as a brothel at a miner's camp—though not in that way exactly, don't get me wrong.

Nudelman leaned back in his chair and gave me that loose grin that hadn't changed much since the first time I saw him that day at Bolton High. I still remember the words, "C'mon, I'll show you around." He mushed his words, still does, and I didn't know what "c'mon" meant but I soon got used to his speech. It's American, I later decided, informal and direct. What's a consonant among friends after all? He was the first one of my classmates at Bolton High to reach out to me after the War Refugee people dropped me in Bolton straight from the D.P. camp.

That night in my book-lined apartment at the Center I worked late, drafting a well-reasoned persuasive explanation of the advantages of the boarding school. But as it turned out I wouldn't use it. So much for battle plans.

# THREE

# The Talk of Elders

There we were, the five old folks and me, seated at the heavy black oak dining table in the cavernous dining hall with its peaked roof supported by massive cross beams. Through the tall gothic windows on both sides of the hall I could see bibulous white clouds and the tops of old chestnut trees swaying in the autumn wind like praying Jews. It was cold in the vast room—a cold that had been stored for years—and we seemed so fragile and insignificant, as if the room had been designed for Goliath.

Remnants of a gentler naive time, the old folks sat in a line, expectant, their faces shrunken, wrinkled, distended, beautiful, faintly lit with the satisfaction that they had been recognized. Most of the time they were overlooked like a picture in a dark corner that has hung quietly for forty years. Their functions in Bolton had either been taken on by others or were no longer needed. Among them was the owner of what we used to call a hamburger joint; an antiques dealer (there was no branch of the Salvation Army in Bolton); a door-to-door household goods salesman ("Dollar down a dollar a week!"); a mother of two sons, both killed in World War II; and a high school teacher.

Selma Novik, the matriarch, was frail, almost transparent, as if her body would one day disintegrate, leaving only her soul. Her blue, deep-set eyes were those of a child peeking out of the Halloween mask of an old, wrinkled lady. Next to her was Izzy Bortz—owl-like behind his post-cataract magnifying glass lenses, a deck of cards on the table in front of him.

Gene Karp was eyeing me from under his still-black, barbed wire-like eyebrows, with his characteristic suspicion. Then there was Susana Leventhal, the first woman high school teacher in the county. Her age was either 101 or 98 depending on whom you talked to—she was no longer sure. Miss Leventhal, as she was still called, was sitting erect as she always had in class; she was a stickler for good posture. Steel grey hair, what there was of it, was neatly knotted on top of her head.,. Her clackers, too perfect to be real, just showed through the opening of her tight lipless mouth. Her eyes looking alternately vacant and alert suggested that her mind was living in two places at once. Maimonides Kravitz looked sanguine and self-possessed, with a much-thumbed copy of the *Atlantic Monthly* and an anthology of poetry by Milosz open in front of him. His many-colored *keepah,* a mystical vision of paradise, sat perched on his shiny, bald head. He acknowledged me with a curious and warm look.

I sat down, feeling at ease and glad to be among them. Except for a cousin in Israel I had no family, so the old folks were as close as I could come to knowing their generation. Aside from that, they were as comforting as an old quilt on a winter night. Being with them is a glimpse of what's ahead for all of us.

There was a pot of tea on the table, brown stoneware with a top that didn't fit. Chipped but indestructible china mugs, and a pile of Russian tea biscuits filled with cherry jelly and walnuts baked by Selma Novik completed the service. Remarkably self-sufficient, the seniors shared much of the daily chores other than the housecleaning. As Maimonides liked to say, "We don't want to put people out."

The old folks lived almost in a state of grace. No one had died among them in the last ten years. True, there had been a little corrective surgery now and then but what old garment doesn't need a patch or two. Dr. Zucker was out there three times a week, and they consumed so many pills that the Purity Drug Store might have closed down without them.

"So, Mendel, what brings you out here on such a blustery day?" Selma asked, as if I had come by foot on a long journey rather than five minutes out of town in a car. Implicit in her question was the premise that few people came to visit.

"I longed for a good conversation," I said.

"A good conversation is like sweet butter," said Kravitz.

"Schnapps is better," said Bortz, riffling his cards.

Kravitz gave me a look that said, don't mind him. "When I was your age, Mendel, we used to talk till dawn over tea." He was the only one who hadn't been born in Bolton, having come from Brest-Litovsk in 1919, and he still spoke with a little Slavic twist of the tongue.

"Now there's the all-night TV movies if you can't sleep," said Karp.

"Trash!" said Kravitz, not unkindly.

"Your garbage is my gold," rejoined Bortz, his laser lenses pointed at his adversary.

"Never argue with a fool!" said Kravitz and he shook his head with a bemused smile.

"They go on that way sometimes, Mendel," Selma said. "It happens when you live day after day with somebody. Habits get on your nerves. It takes tolerance, which we have of course."

"How are you getting along?" I asked, still unwilling to put the subject on the table.

Kravitz shrugged. "Every day is a blessing!"

"A gift," said Miss Leventhal. "When you get to a certain age, every day is a gift." Her head shook a little, as did her voice when she spoke. She flicked a few crumbs of the tea cake off of her brown shawl.

I remembered how old she had seemed that first frightening year at Bolton High and how nervous I had been the day she asked me to recite some Wordsworth. Not that I didn't know it, but I was afraid the others would snicker at my Polish accent. To put me at my ease she had announced to the class that I could speak five languages, all of them fluently, and that Josef Conrad, a Pole, had written all of his novels in English. Nobody laughed.

"Do you get bored out here?" I asked, leading toward the topic of my visit.

"Never! There's always something to do," said Selma, and in turn they catalogued their interests and activities. Selma watched birds, kept a record of each siting, cooked, baked, and sewed. Kravitz read and wrote. Currently he was grinding away at a monograph on Duns Scotus and Herman Hesse. Miss Leventhal played the piano when she had the energy. Izzy Bortz and Gene Karp played cards, watched television, and kept the place from falling apart; both were handy with tools.

"Would you believe it, Mendel?" said Selma, gesturing toward Bortz. "He has rewired the fuse box, himself?"

"I almost electrocuted myself, but I did it," said Bortz shaking his hand.

"Isn't this place just too big for you?" I asked.

"No, we love the space. Each of us can be alone when we want to," said Miss Leventhal. Her voice had grown younger with age and was childlike, but the articulation was precise as ever.

None of my reasons for ultimately suggesting that they share the building with a school was reaching them. "Do you miss having children about?" I threw out hopefully.

"I had enough of children," said Karp, swinging his hand with contempt, "with all that noise, and always spilling things."

"Don't mind him," said Selma. "Everybody loves having children around, even Gene Karp."

"God communicates through the faces of children," said Maimonides Kravitz.

"Then I have good news. You'll be having children all around you soon. The Board has decided to create a Jewish boarding school." I tried to make it sound auspicious and looked at each of their faces.

It took a few seconds for the message to register and each took it differently. Miss Leventhal began to glow. Izzy Bortz contracted an advanced stage of gangrene. The rest seemed as though they were about to try a new cake recipe.

"Where?" said Izzy.

"Here."

"Where do we go?" Izzy sounded hurt and he began to automatically wipe the table in front of him with his crumpled napkin.

"You stay here. Of course you may have to move to another room, since we'll be putting up some walls to separate the dormitory from your quarters."

"Move from my room? But I like my room," said Izzy Bortz, drawing in his drooping lower lip.

"It will be just as big, with the same view of the grounds."

"But it won't be my room. And what about the noise and the tumult?" said Karp.

Selma and Maimonides seemed to be getting used to the idea, glancing at each other with questions in their eyes. Afraid to say any more, I zipped my lip. What if they raised a fuss, wrote to the Grey Panthers, or even worse, the newspaper. I picked up the rest of my tea cake and bit into it. The room was so quiet, my chewing resounded in my head like a meat grinder. Maimonides raised his eyebrows and took a deep, wheezy breath before he reached for another tea cake.

"I think it's just a wonderful idea, Mendel," Selma finally said. "After all, this place is empty. It should be put to use. And it would give us something more to do than watch the paint peel off of the walls."

"I agree," said Kravitz, and his Adam's apple bounced as he swallowed.

"It's positively exciting!" said Miss Leventhal.

My heart began to beat in my ears with relief.

"Yes, you'll even help with the classes if you like," I said. "They will be like grandchildren to you and the teachers will provide adult learning, learning for the elderly, all sorts of courses. It will be stimulating, a new lease on life."

"My old lease hasn't expired yet," said Bortz.

"It sounds like heaven." Selma.

"I'll teach poetry," said Miss Leventhal and the look she gave me was full of a common recollection of my days in her class.

"And I will teach the Baal Shem Tov," Maimonides said.

"Izzy Bortz will teach poker," said Karp, pointing at the cards. And Bortz answered, "Karp will teach them how to cheat."

"Will we eat together as well?"

"Yes, if you like, but we plan to set up a separate sitting room for you and the faculty, just to have quiet. And there will be a table in there and comfortable chairs."

"Yes, that's good. I like that. What about the bathrooms?" Selma asked.

"You won't have to share."

"Good. That's important." Selma nodded and poured some more tea.

"So you agree?"

"And if we didn't, what then?" Izzy Bortz was smiling now, a dill pickle smile, but a smile all the same.

"Even so, the Board wants to know."

"Well, tell the Board, we'll make the best of it." Izzy Bortz folded his hands over his flabby stomach.

"More than that, Mendel. I'm looking forward to it," said Selma.

"I hope there won't be a lot of carpenters around. I can't stand hammering and those electric saws. It's like they are sawing inside your head."

"Mendel, before you go, let me give you two of my tea cakes. I know how much you like them. Do you think the children will as well?"

"Selma," I said. "I'm sure the tea cakes will make you the most popular person at the school."

# FOUR

# A Faithful Friend

Estelle had thought of selling the house many times, but she couldn't bring herself to. What would she do with all the furniture, all the stuff that filled the drawers and closets? Sometimes, late at night if she couldn't sleep, she would pick a drawer or a closet and browse. At these times she wished that she had kept a journal, even though the pages would have been filled with tuna casseroles and scrambled eggs, and poems written by their friends in celebration of their twentieth wedding anniversary. Sydney was gone; her son Noah was practicing psychotherapy in Pittsburgh. She had a grandchild now, Ariel. Noah, Monica and Ariel came down for the weekend often enough. When they did, the house was full again and echoes of the friendly chaos of a young family's life carried her to the next visit.

She would tell me this and more. Estelle told me everything. I was her counselor, her confessor, and through her I lived the surrogate life of a father and grandfather. I told her everything as well. Almost everything. I had never told her that

I loved her, more than as my closest friend; but I couldn't bring myself to say it. Even after all these years, to say that I wanted her, as a woman, would somehow adulterate Sidney, which was foolish and irrational. (Is that proper English: *adultery* therefore *adulterate*? I must look it up in the dictionary later.) Somehow, I always had the feeling of Sidney's presence, of the curl of cigar smoke coming through the half open door of his den. I couldn't imagine being in bed with Estelle, not in her bed at least. But I could see myself waking up, rolling over and bumping into Sidney. So, there we were, the two of us, living today but stuck in the cobweb of the past.

In truth I had missed my chance. Nudelman was a jumper. I was a hesitator. Some years after Sidney's death, Estelle had asked me to move in with her—as a boarder of course, but I refused, tempting though it might have been. Later I regretted refusing but she had never asked again, and I assumed she had lost interest.

Then came my so-called medical leave to Canyon Springs, California and my fling with Sarah Cavanaugh. That spun me in a different direction and, I guess, put Estelle off. When I came back from Canyon Springs she was welcoming, and we saw a lot of each other. I was there several times a week for dinner and often dropped in for morning coffee. We went to plays and concerts in Pittsburgh at least once a month and always had dinner before. Sometimes we held hands like teenagers, but nothing more. I suppose I was afraid of disappointing her. After all, I was no Casanova. On the other hand, I wasn't exactly a monk. I had a physical, even sensual side, if you will, and lately I had even begun to flirt with the national craze of jogging. Understand I had never been chubby, but I had an aversion to these middle-aged men who begin to look a little pregnant just about the time that their wives don't.

If Estelle knew about the nameless widow from McKeesport, she never mentioned it. Heda Finkelstein knows all and tells all. Now that I think of it, Estelle asked once what I did every Sunday night and I recall brushing the question aside with an embarrassed chuckle and cursing Heda Finkelstein, in my head of course.

Here we were, the two of us in that perfect dream of middle America: the Casa Cantor, colonial in its decor right down to the pin cushion, except for the green copper menorah on the maple buffet; an incongruous novelty that Sidney had picked up on one of his Jewish Welfare Board missions to Israel. Would that I could have given her my mother's three-hundred-year-old silver menorah with the two rampant lions holding up the *shammes* candle, but that was only a sweet painful memory. So now there was this candelabrum, perched on its spindly legs and still holding the candles, like Israel itself.

Estelle was just emerging from the kitchen, a glass coffee pot extended forward like a handgun. Food is a weapon after all. She has changed very little over the years, to my eyes at least. Estelle is not a tall woman, although she has a presence in the way she holds her head, a little high, so that some people might take her to be haughty when she is only trying to make the best of her five-foot three stature and keep her breasts from sagging. Her eyes are on the dark side of mahogany, so that you have to get close to see the nuance and texture of her irises, and they are acute and animated, revealing a lively, critical, but caring mind. Her eyes are just as big as the first time I saw her next to her locker at Bolton High, but the little creases all around them give away the number of years they've been looking at the world. Her most striking feature is her eyebrows, shaped exactly like the wings of a gull in flight. Her hair is thick and the rich auburn highlights that I remember are beginning to fade, now that the grey is starting to intrude. She's been talking about "touching it up." She's also a good dresser, and the taupe silk blouse and black wool slacks favored her shape, but I'm no fashion editor.

OK, she was older than she used to be. So am I. Even so, there is something magical about growing old. As a snake sheds its skin, we are slowly replaced by another person, resembling us more than a little, but certainly not the same, yet close enough and slowly enough that we don't go out of our mind. What if we woke up one day, say on our sixtieth birthday, and found that we were old. What then?

Outside, it was raining hard and the wind was making a little tattoo on the window and sighing in the nearly bare trees. We had just finished the apricot crisp, and I was feeling pleasantly full—Estelle never serves over-sized portions.

"No butter!" she exclaimed. And the dried apricots are sulfur-free."

"I feel better already, doctor. I think I shall live forever. Well, at least longer than I had planned to."

"Seriously, Mendel, how is your cholesterol. Have you had it checked?"

"Yes, I am pleased to announce that it is 50-percent butterfat, which is good."

"Be serious, Mendel. You should be aware of such things."

She poured some coffee into the Limoges china cup, not colonial—an heirloom from her mother—and sat down, bending toward me.

"So you were telling me about the boarding school."

"You should be on the Board, Estelle. It would be good for you."

"I've got enough to do, Mendel. You know how it is, the busy never have enough time."

Estelle was still fixated on the stock market and doing well with the insurance money and the little she had recovered from the sale of the business. But it took a lot of time, buying and selling, selling and buying, hedging, putting and taking, optioning and futuring and all that.

"In your next life, maybe you'll be a what-do-they-call-it, a barb, the ones who bet on companies taking each other over?"

"You mean an arb, from *arbitrage*."

"More like *abattoir*."

"Never mind the market, I get enough of that. The school!" Estelle has a high, nasal voice, but I rather like it. It keeps you on your toes, you could say.

I raised my hand and fluttered my fingers, something my father used to do.

"It comes."

"The gossip, Mendel. Do I have to get it all from Heda Finkelstein?"

"There is no gossip, only facts. We have applications for teachers; some look OK but not enough. The same can be said about the students. The carpenters are disturbing Izzy Bortz."

Months had passed since the Board had given Nudelman the green light. Months full of details, what with architect's plans, building contracts, permit applications, budgets, mailings and so on. And this was just the beginning. There was still the search for teachers and a director to be faced. After all, not everyone would put a position in Bolton on par with one in Cleveland or Pittsburgh. Nudelman's patience was beginning to wear thin, and he had the tenacity of a pit bull.

"Izzy Bortz was always a complainer," said Estelle. "I remember the time he kicked us all out of his hamburger joint because Nudelman put an open bottle of beer on the counter."

"We were so naive, then. What did we know from hard drugs? Drugs were aspirin. Coke, you could have at the fountain with cherry or chocolate. Remember the soda fountain at the... What was it called?"

"Mary's Confectionary."

"The stools with little backs. You could swivel around, and they would bring you back to center."

"They tore it down after Mary died." Estelle got that dreamy look, then she turned to me with amusement and said, "She was so fat. And remember, she didn't have any eyebrows. She used to paint them on. She looked like a kewpie doll."

"Yes. Like a clown."

"Remember we used to place bets on whether she would get wedged behind the counter. Wait. I want to show you something." She got up and went to the kitchen, returning in a moment with a heavy glass dish shaped like a banana. She handed it to me with a look of pride. "I found it at a rummage sale. There were six of them on the shelf."

"I must confess something, Estelle. I've never had a banana split in my life, never," I said, brandishing the bowl.

"I don't believe it."

"Who could afford thirty-five cents?"

"I'll make you one some-ay."

"I led a deprived childhood."

"You were talking about the school."

"The old folks are surviving, even looking forward to it, except for Karp and maybe Bortz. Just what I told you the last time. Why are you so curious? Do you want a job or are you planning to endow a classroom, which you don't have to do as there is so much money in the Mossberg Trust."

And that's how it was with us.

# FIVE

# Red Star in the East

L ife is an endless paper chain of compromises, you could say. As children we equate our aspirations with what is fair. But life is not always fair, any more than we—you and me—always do the right thing, making the right choice when we have a choice, and meeting the expectations of people who depend on us. Life comes at you like a drunk driver. It's nothing you planned, and if you had thought it was going to happen you would have gotten out of the way.

Sorry about that! You wanted to know what was going on with the school and I drop a wet rag on your face. But what I said has something to do with the school, you see, because as the Board plodded forward and the momentous start of the first academic year closed in on us, we were all seized by icy panic. Nothing was as we hoped it would be. One phase of the work was going well, at least, the minor structural changes in the main building had been completed. But enrolment and teacher recruitment were falling short, and worst of all, none of the people who had applied for the post of Director looked good enough.

The day of the momentous Board meeting it was raining cats and rats, a smothering August rain. The whole town was drooping, the trees forlorn with weighted leaves, showing the fatigue of a hot summer. A yellow poster from last spring's county fair, blistered and peeling, clung to the window of the army surplus store at the wrong end of Main Street. Children, looking like runaway fire hydrants in their bright yellow slickers and rain hats, splashed through puddles on the way to visit friends.

The mood around the Board table was like the taste of milk gone sour. Fourteen synagogue presidents looked down from the wall, spectators at a losing game. Raincoats, limp and smelling of mildew, were draped over the spare chairs. Water was still trickling down Finkelstein's wrinkled forehead from his soaked hair. The rest were waiting, sipping coffee from Styrofoam cups. Rabbi Bing was making notes, probably for his next sermon, and between thoughts chatting with Steve Roe. Looking ahead to the winter, Sophie Feld was knitting something brown while Harriet Rosenzweig skimmed the *New Republic*.

If Nudelman was worried he didn't show it. It was his baby and he was bound to feel good about it no matter how it turned out. He watched Finkelstein settle into his chair then opened his file and fanned out the letters, as diverse in their appearance as the applicants.

"Good news!" he said, with the sincerity of a master salesman. "I think we have found our director!"

"None too soon," said Rabbi Bing, polishing his thick glasses with a clean handkerchief and looking like a mole.

"Yes, and you'll be surprised although there is a downside."

"Surprise us!" said Finkelstein.

Nudelman picked up a clipped sheaf of papers and flourished it with the air of a momentous announcement; a war had ended, or one had begun. "I think our director has been located."

"Where's he been?" quipped Finkelstein through a summer cold.

"Moscow."

"Not a Refusenik! Are you nuts?" shrieked Finkelstein.

"Yes, a Refusenik! It'll put us on the map!"

"Nudelman, you're losing it," said Roe.

"Hear him out," said Rabbi Bing, now back in focus.

"Thank you. You'll be glad. First off, he speaks English and Hebrew, and he's a pedagogue by profession."

"Good, then he likes little boys!" Finkelstein again. Don't get him wrong. He wasn't the kind who gripes about everything, just the type who had to get his word in all the time on every subject.

"Not a pederast! May I go on?"

"Go."

"His name is Lev Kyol." Nudelman repeated it, trying to get the pronunciation right. "He's been the director of an elementary school in Moscow. He's now in Vienna."

"What could he possibly know about Jewish education? They send people to Siberia for having a study group." Sophie Feld looked up from her knitting to ask this in her languid tone.

"His grandfather was a famous rabbi."

"So hire his grandfather," persisted Finkelstein. "You think knowledge comes by osmosis? You'll make fools of the community, Nudelman."

Nudelman's face was getting red. He picked up a few of the letters, shook them and said in a tight voice, "That would be unnecessary, in your case, at least. Look, I've written 30 letters, made 20 phone calls, gone through 35 applications, and this is the only one that comes close to what we want."

Harriet Rosenzweig looked up from her magazine. "A sad commentary on the state of Jewish education."

"Look, Bolton isn't Los Angeles. Not every rising educator would think of Bolton as advancing his career—no offence to you, Rabbi Bing or you, Mendel." Steve Roe was probably thinking back on his move from Hartford, Connecticut.

"So what's wrong with Bolton, Steve?" said Finkelstein.

"Please let him finish." Rabbi Bing swept the room with his gaze.

And finish he did. An hour later the Board was convinced, or rather resigned, or more to the point rationalized. We would hire the Refusenik for a year and if he didn't work out, at least he would have gotten to America, and we'd have a year to find somebody else.

"Are you satisfied, Nudelman?" I asked, as we walked out of the room together.

"Satisfied? Why?"

"You got what you wanted, didn't you?"

"This isn't what I wanted, Mendel, but life is a series of compromises." And with that he rushed ahead of me into the rain. I never found out just what would have suited him.

## SIX

# The Kettle and the Crock

The boardroom was full and buzzing with excited conversation. There were real glass tea and coffee cups on the buffet—no Styrofoam—and the usual assortment of home-baked cakes and cookies. After all these years I knew who had made each. The crowd was, for the most part, made up of the school board and their families, as well as other community leaders, such as Dr. Zucker. It was their first look at the new director and only his second day in town. Nudelman had picked him up at the Pittsburgh airport only the day before.

Lev Kyol was a tall, angular man, weathered as an unpainted barn; his clothes were shabby, drab as a cloudy winter day. In so many words he resembled one of those anonymous men who spend their lives hunched in a newspaper kiosk. And yet, in spite of his humble appearance, he exuded an aura of self-possession and strength.

"Kyol, Lyew," he said to each person, extending a long arm with a firm squeeze, a grip that wouldn't let go while he possessed you with his stony grey eyes. And he repeated his name with his smoky rough voice that was, all the same, mellifluous and soft in the vowels, twisting the "l" into a pretzel and whirling the "y" from his wisdom teeth. It was a pleasant sound, his voice and accent, one that would get and hold attention because it was different.

He was facing Finkelstein, Rabbi Bing, and Steve Roe and saying something I couldn't hear. People kept turning from the cookies and their conversations toward him with a mixture of curiosity and pride of possession. They might have been showing off the features of a new car. And he was looking back with surprising familiarity, as if he had known these people all of his life and had a perfect right to be where he was.

From the beginning I felt a kinship with him. Years ago I had faced the same jury of kind but strange faces, and I thought of my apprehension that snowy day in 1947 when I got off the Greyhound bus in Bolton as a teenage refugee, trying to identify a sponsor whom I had never met. But I was just a kid then while Lev Kyol was an adult of 50 or so years, with who knows how many experiences behind him. Not that my war years had been a prolonged summer camp. Anything but.

I was, as usual, standing a little apart, the better to observe Lev's thin grey hair, combed the long way across a flat skull, the pronounced cheekbones and the hollowed, thin skin of his face. Add a sharp, rather droopy nose, with thin nostrils to keep out the winter air, thin lips that turned up a little at the ends and red ears that stood out a bit from his head, and the usual wear and tear wrinkles of course.

As I stood there sipping my tea, watching the members of the Board compete for his attention and size him up, his head slowly turned my way and I was floodlit by his sudden gaze. There was warmth, understanding and a sprinkle of bemusement in it that mirrored my own feelings. I had barely met the man and already knew him. It was the mattress ticking of friendship and more often romance and I tucked it away and promised myself to speak to him when the others had lost interest.

I put my tea cup down and walked around the Board table to eavesdrop on the talk. It was the sort that goes on at receptions, a few self-conscious and self-evident questions directed at the newcomer, a pleasant response from him and a moment of lapse while they search for something more to say before parting with a smile and a nod. Now it was only Rabbi Bing who was speaking with him.

The rabbi had in fact made the final decision after a telephone interview with Kyol. "He knows his stuff," Rabbi Bing had said. The rabbi had prepared some pointed questions to test Kyol's knowledge. It seems that Lev had managed to retain some of his grandfather's Judaic library.

"And he even has some good ideas about education. He's very articulate and his English is surprisingly fluent. He tells me he's the author of a manuscript, unpublished, on the impact of Hassidism on the Anarchistic aspects of the Russian Revolution. Astonishing!" The rabbi had reported to the Board, looking a little awed and envious.

Nudelman sidled up to me, poked me on the chest with the curved bit of his pipe. "What do you think?"

"I—"

Another poke. "You know, Estelle Cantor is letting him stay in her house, for the time being, until his apartment is finished at the home. I mean, the school."

This took me by surprise. "She didn't tell me."

"My doing, Mendel. I just set it up this morning."

"I've got to hand it to you, Nudelman. No grass grows on you."

"Tomorrow, he'll start interviewing the rest of the teachers, you know. It's best that we let him take over right away, subject to the personnel committee's review, of course."

"Of course. Has Estelle met him yet?"

"No. I'm going to take him over there after this little shindig."

"I'll take him," I hastened to offer. "You should get back to work."

Nudelman squeezed my arm. "Do I smell—"

"What?"

"Nothing, Mendel. Nothing." And off he went to talk to the rabbi, dropping ashes from his pipe on the brown asbestos tile.

Lev Kyol leaned forward in the seat of my old Chevy and began fingering the knobs and instruments of the dash like a child. Again, it was raining—one of the wettest summers anyone could remember. The windshield wipers were slapping and smearing leaving the usual blur at eye level. The only time when I remember to replace the wipers is when I need them and then of course it's raining.

"This is very good car!" Lev said, running his finger across the radio.

"It's just an old gas guzzler. You should see the new ones."

"This everything what you need. Radio. Heater. Wipers work. Not stolen like in Soviet Union."

"You should see the new ones. They even have air bags to keep you alive in a crash."

"How do you have time to get inside?

"Inside what?"

"Air bag."

That was funny, I thought. He has a sense of humor on top of it all, unless he wasn't joking.

"Here everyone has a car!" he said, looking at me with childish wonder as if to imply that if someone like me, with the wages of a dislocated elevator operator, had one, America was truly El Dorado.

"In Soviet Union, pedagogue would not have car. A little hut in country next to garden maybe, but car, no."

"Here it's a necessity. You would die waiting for a public bus in Bolton."

"Why is that?"

"Because everybody has a car, I suppose," thinking my explanation was oxymoronic, maybe.

"Terrible waste."

"It's liberating in a way."

"People should walk more. Walking is good."

"All the same you'll soon want one of your own, Lev."

"Soon I too will be American, is that what you are saying?"

We were on Main Street. The windows had steamed up and he rubbed a circle with his hand to get a better look.

"So many shops," he said.

"You should see the shopping center out on Freestone Road."

"How many shops do you need?"

"There are no rules."

"When I become American, I will understand?" he said with an ironic shade in his smoky voice.

"Yes, whatever it is to be an American. A car is a big part of it."

"I have nothing with me, you know, nothing but my grandfather's books."

"He was a famous rabbi?"

"Not exactly famous but respected in his town."

"Was it a big town?"

"Not very big. Small I would call it. A tavern, a *shul,* a store, a church, a police station, there you have it all, that and houses."

"All the fixtures of society." I know it wasn't proper, but my curiosity got the better of my discretion and I decided to pry some more biography out of him.

"You came here from Moscow. Were you brought up in Moscow?"

"During Great War I lived in Novosibirsk. You know it?"

"Not really."

"My father was bricklayer. He built housing blocks. My mother was seamstress. She sewed uniforms for Army. I went to school, joined young Communist. *Komsomol,* you know, like Boy Scouts. I had older sister, Katya, a teacher. After war we go back to Moscow, my father do same work until he get pneumonia, chest sickness, from working outside in cold, building houses like Socialist hero, and he die. I was in school to become teacher."

"What about your sister?"

"She get teaching job in Khabarovsk, far away. I seldom see her. My mother die...died, two year after my father, heart attack. She remained sad since he die...died."

A car stopped suddenly in front of me and I jammed on the brakes throwing him forward. "You should put your seat belt on," I said.

"Yes," he said, fumbling with the strap.

And with the seat belt our friendship began, quite at random. Despite the weather I drove a little faster, eager to observe the impression Lev Kyol would make on Estelle. It was, of course, ridiculous but I was feeling just a little jealous that this utter newcomer should share her home. A rival? Hardly a rival, but all the same.

It was obvious from the way she looked at him that Estelle was interested in this gangling, intense school director and it was not just that it would be nice to have a Refusenik around to talk about how things are in Moscow, whether it's colder there than in Bolton, and so on.

"They say the weather in Moscow is abominable in the winter," she said, passing him a basket piled high with fresh raisin and cinnamon scones. We were sitting around the table in the warmth of the kitchen. It was raining harder and the windows around the bay were steamy and streaked.

As with the car, Lev was astonished at the display of possessions and space. By the look of him he must be thinking that Estelle was one of the Rockefeller grandchildren to have such a house. But he would find out that it was no better than the home of any of her friends. "No more than the standard 2400 square feet," as Sidney used to say.

"Estelle, have you done something to your hair?" I asked, studying the more uniform brown shade.

"Do you like it, Mendel?" She raised her hand to touch it.

Don't tell me she had somehow colored the sprinkle of grey! Why on earth!

"Yes, it's very complementary to the shape of your face."

"The weather. Worse it gets, more we like it. Some Muscovites say not only is cold good for circulation, it kills all germs."

"If it doesn't kill them it must slow them down," said Estelle, offering him more tea.

"Or drive them inside," I said.

"Such fresh butter!" he said spreading about a quarter of an inch on the flat side of his scone. "In Soviet Union butter taste little like cheese."

That's how relationships begin: talking of weather and germs. Who knows, maybe that's what Adam and Eve first talked about when they met the snake. The apple came later.

# SEVEN

# Guide to the Perplexed

When things are going well it's time to hold your breath. Don't step on cracks and stay away from ladders. As my uncle Mayer used to say, "Chance is a question of luck." I know, it's oxymoronic (again) but I had to share it, and in fact, when you give it some thought, it's even a little profound.

In the short time between Lev Kyol's coming and the beginning of the school year, everything fell into place like the last pieces of a puzzle. In fact he didn't have as much to do as I had thought. Most of the teachers, who had been given offers, accepted.

Unfortunately, as with Lev, the committee had to rely on reference verification and telephone interviews but they had pictures and plenty of documentation. Compromises were made but it was, after all, only the first year. The same applied to the students. If there were no Einsteins among them, neither were there dunces, judging by their records, although more than a few of them were certified troublemakers. It was to be expected that parents might think a boarding school would straighten out their children's bent characters, although a child is not a fender, and a school is not a body shop.

As for my role, I had become Lev's guide, and I was enjoying interpreting America to a complete stranger. People said Russians tended to be enthusiastic feeling types, and Lev was no exception. When he wasn't at work on the curriculum, racing through textbooks, or cramming American History like a college freshman, he wanted to take in everything. His questions landed with the frequency of robins in the spring and ranged from the supermarket shelves to the incongruities of wealth against the shadow of want.

I took him to K-Mart at the shopping center and he wouldn't leave. All the power tools, saws, sanders, electric lawn mowers, fascinated him. He picked up a little battery-powered drill and said, "Is this for a dentist?"

I read the box. "It's just to have around the house—for convenience, holes for cup hooks."

"Convenience. A way of life here."

Outside, we strolled along the row of shops passing the One Day Cleaner and the One Day Film Developer.

"What is hurry?"

"People don't like to wait when they want something."

"Like a crying baby," he said.

Of all that he saw, the abundance continued to amaze him. For example, I took him on a driving tour of Bolton, to see not only the newer ranch-style homes on the hilly edge of town where the doctors and shop owners lived, but also the older stout brick houses closer to the river, with front porches crowding narrow streets and roofs like party hats.

He told me that the town must be full of millionaires, for "nobody, not even the Party Chairman lives in free-standing house in Soviet Union."

When he learned that the one on Second Avenue, with the new grey aluminum siding, belonged to Caz Koslowski, who drove a forklift at the mill, and the yellow brick house on Third Avenue, with the camper parked in the drive, belonged to Chuck Crenshaw, an assistant manager at the A & P, he accused me of filling him with propaganda. He wasn't convinced until I let him pick a house at random and we climbed the steps to the porch and rang the bell.

A woman wearing pink plastic rollers in her hair responded. She spoke to us through the oxidized aluminum screen door but was friendly enough. I improvised some questions. Her husband was a tire salesman. They had two of everything: two kids, two TVs, two cars. Even two mortgages. It was an American Noah's Ark. Then and only then did he realize that Bolton was no Potemkin village.

"But Mendel, show me where the homeless live."

"I can't."

"Why not?"

I explained that they lived in the cities. I wanted to say that even the homeless leave Bolton .

Insisting that I show him the poor we drove along Front Street past a row of crummy bars and one or two drab hotels where pensioners and winos existed. He was reassured to see shabby men leaning against the wall with nothing to do but suck wine out of rumpled paper bags.

"In Soviet Union everybody has job, not that they work. They stand on street a lot too, in line to buy food." Again, there was the hint of irony in his voice.

Of all the impressions of life in America, the supermarket was the one that blew him away, as the kids say. The first time, he must have spent two hours just looking. He kept picking things up, smelling them, shaking them to make sure they were real. In the end, after all that fingering and poking, what do you think he bought? Polish sausage and a pound of potatoes.

In the next two weeks I saw him often, for Estelle was cooking dinner for him and I usually included myself, even when she didn't call to invite me. She had taken a fancy to him; it was obvious. She tried to please him with all of her specialties: apricot-peach pie, pigs in a blanket, and a lot of heavy, Eastern European recipes, like *cholent*, passed down from her mother but out of fashion in our cholesterol-conscious society. I must confess that I was becoming Di-Gel dependent—I just wasn't used to the heavy, fat-laden food.

"In winter you need fat to keep out cold," Lev said, mortaring his slab of freshly baked challah with a quarter of an inch of sweet butter and topping his bowl of thick borscht with a dollop of real sour cream, not the low-fat kind.

Estelle watched him, glowing like a rose at twilight. Was there more than hospitality here, I wondered. She was doing everything a young bride would do for him: washing his clothes, even folding and putting them away in his drawers. She bought him pressurized shaving cream and a cartridge razor, which fascinated him. He began to smell of Bay Rum—not the kind you drink, what you put on your face.

"You sure are making Lev welcome," I said after dinner one night as I dried the dishes. He had gone up to his room to work. A tireless worker; according to Estelle, he sometimes went to bed at dawn—but how would she know?

"It's nice to have a man in the house to do for." A smile came into her eyes; full of memories for her dead husband, I assumed, and I again regretted not having taken up her offer to move in with her.

"How is he to live with?"

"Quiet as a cat. And clean. He likes long soaks in the bathtub, says it's a luxury. We live like royalty, he keeps telling me." She touched her finger to her lip. "He's very helpful—takes out the trash, washes dishes. He even repaired that short in the table lamp. He's handy."

"What's he do all of the time?"

"I think he's doing a syllabus for the school. He's got all of the textbooks and he's been poring over them."

This was interesting, and I wondered if he'd shared any of his work with the education committee of the Board. "Has he been meeting with the Board?" I asked.

With moderate reproof in her eyes she said, "Really, Mendel, I'm not his secretary, just his housekeeper."

"But you must see—"

"He goes for long walks, I don't know where. Although, several times, he'd walked out to the old folks' home…I should say the school."

"Really!"

"It's only a few miles, although it was in the rain! He seems very hardy for—"

"For what?"

"A Refusenik. You know, bad food, no sun, no exercise."

Hardy indeed. "Does he talk much?"

"Oh, we have long conversations. He knows so much about everything."

"Does he watch TV?"

"Occasionally."

"Hm. Is there anything bad about him?" I asked, feeling like the FBI.

"He gets terrible headaches." She nodded, looking like she had one herself.

"At least he's human. When's he moving to his new quarters?"

"Next week, just before the faculty is supposed to arrive."

"That's good."

"Why?""Good for the school, I mean. He'll be right there where he's needed."

"Yes, I suppose so." she said, and her forehead wrinkled for a moment.

# EIGHT

# Calling the Lost Sheep

Looking across the dining hall at Nudelman made me think of all the famous people who, for the first time, saw their visions crystalize. Edison for example, when the wire in the glass sphere began to give off light, or Washington, as he looked about during his inauguration, thinking perhaps about how far he had come and awed and sobered by the obstacles and uncertainties that faced him. Of course, an institution, like a state or a school, is never realized. Every day it changes, becoming something—more or less but different—until, sometimes, it is unrecognizable in substance and form, as different from its origins as the infant is from the octogenarian he becomes.

If there was any apprehension in Nudelman's bones the day the Board welcomed the faculty of the school, I couldn't see it. Pride, satisfaction, and an erect confidence shone in his eyes. He was almost as rumpled as always, and ashes dropped from his pipe as he spoke to Mr. Harney, the new Hebrew and Jewish Studies teacher. Harney looked more like a bricklayer than a teacher. His face was tan, sun-wrinkled. His nose was flat, and his jaw protruded, giving him the look of a tenacious bulldog. Add to that the biceps and forearms of a weightlifter attached to a body that was barely five foot three.

It's a distortion to focus on Nudelman when there was so much to see and digest. The great dining hall for instance was cheered by fresh paint on the walls above the dark wood wainscot. The wood frames of the high gothic windows glistened with fresh varnish. Only the heavy crossbeams of the pitched ceiling were untouched, perhaps to provide some continuity. All of the round iron chandeliers had been dusted and the many bulbs replaced. The white cloths on the tables and glasses full of local orange marigolds gave the cathedral-like room a bright festive look. Add to that the bubbling drone of voices animated by Gene Karp's secret rum punch, and a blue and white banner stretched across the stage proclaiming "Welcome Tikva School Faculty," and you have the setting for the most momentous event in the history of Bolton since the fire station burned down. Tikva, by the way, was the name of the school—it means hope.

Little did I know how momentous it would be, but this was before Lev Kyol had given his so-called inaugural address. I sipped the rum punch—it was so strong I wondered whether Karp had forgotten the original formula—and approached Miss Leventhal and Selma Novik. They were sitting side by side against the wall in high back gothic chairs. Selma was wearing a lavender blue silk dress with a lace collar. Her silver hair was tied back, and her deep blue eyes acknowledged me with a kindly indulgence. If there was a dowager baroness of the estate of all ages, she was it.

"Quite an event," I said, taking her hand and kissing it. She was the only person in Bolton who aroused that quaint Polish custom in me. Miss Leventhal's head shook a bit and I imagined that she was feeling excluded. I kissed her hand as well and she rewarded me with the fossil of a coquettish smile.

"How do you find all this?"

"Mendel," said Miss Leventhal, "the school has given us all new life. Every day something new. And we can hardly wait until the children arrive."

"Does everyone feel the same way?" I asked, recalling the skepticism.

"Gene Karp still complains but the rest of us are simply full of expectation," said Selma.

Karp was hardly complaining at the moment. His nose was glowing like a traffic light, no doubt from an excess of his punch.

"These teachers are so interesting to talk to. And so attentive to us. We felt so alone out here and now the world seems to have come to us. People from all over the world with such different experiences."

"Especially that one over there," said Miss Leventhal in her distant quavering voice, and she directed my eye with a finger. "Mr.—"

"Shusterman," I volunteered, looking toward the science teacher, a man who was so thin that he seemed to be made of wire. His hair seemed to be made of wire as well and it looked like a telephone repairman's nightmare.

"And that Mr. Cohen, the new mathematics teacher. Charming!"

"I think it's Cohan"

"You mean like George M. Cohan? He's coming over!"

The man had the demeanor and full white mane of a Shakespearean actor. His nose was monumental, and his cheeks were tracked with red veins. Most striking were his eyes, black and full of feeling, the kind that could burn a hole in an unprepared student.

"The two winter flowers of the garden," he said, seducing each of them in turn with his eyes.

I introduced myself and he met my glance with refreshing warmth. "What are your impressions of the school?"

"I've just arrived of course, but it's an idyllic environment and singular, what with the resident elders as a resource and inspiration. We don't appreciate the past in our society but they will help to teach our students the value of old things and old ways."

"Do you see what I mean, Mendel?" said Selma.

Indeed, I did. In fact, I wondered why we stashed people such as Selma in old folks' closets at all when they had so much to give.

"We consume and waste so much," I said.

Cohan's response was a pained, earnest nod that included me in his as-yet-unspecified view of the world.

The energy in the room was animating and I found myself going  from person to person, exchanging little thoughts and bright homilies like canapés. From the Board I picked up little shreds of disquiet and mystery. It seemed that, after securing a one-year employment contract, Lev Kyol had distanced himself from them, claiming that he must be free to set the school's course, which would explain all those solitary late nights.

I decided to launch into the crowd and seek out the teachers I hadn't yet met. Lyuba Karman, I liked, as soon as she turned her friendly open gaze toward me. A pretty young woman with a broad Slavic face and up-tilted blue eyes, she was the youngest of the teachers, with no more than one year's experience in an inner-city middle school in Chicago. She was from a small town in Indiana and hadn't adjusted to the tough atmosphere, she told me.

Then there was Martin Schweig, who gave me just the opposite reaction. A man in his fifties, he reminded me somehow of a worn-out patio broom. Don't ask me to explain. His expression was as closed as Lyuba's was open. He looked at me as if he were expecting me to disappoint or injure him. What had I done to deserve it? Some people look at the world that way and often the world meets their expectations. I had bad feelings about him and because of that I tried to be friendly.

"I've forgotten, with all the new people, where you are from, Mr. Schweig?"

He seemed to take offense to that. "I've taught all over the country," he said.

"Is there any place that you particularly enjoyed?"

"Not really." I must have looked quizzical for he went on to say, "It's the teaching I enjoy."

"I envy you your commitment." This made him flush as if he wasn't used to being envied. He wasn't the sort you could talk sports with, and I found myself shifting my eyes and sidling away with guilt that I was leaving him standing there alone, and relief that I was getting away from him.

It seemed as though I'd talked to everyone when Nudelman went to the rostrum on the stage and introduced Lev Kyol. Nudelman didn't say much, just something about embarking on a long exploration of familiar and unfamiliar ways.

The room grew palpably still as the director climbed the three steps to the stage, walked with broad strides to the podium and turned his long equine face toward us. He raised his hand and plastered the thin strands of his hair down across his balding head. His nostrils twitched and his ears looked as red as taillights, but his eyes were pools of good feeling as he gazed around the hushed expectant crowd. It was his inaugural address after all.

He spoke without notes: a mark of confidence, or of preparation.

"Friends. Brothers and Sisters." He began. "What is a school, a Jewish school, but a studio to sculpt unformed character and minds of young people? As Jews we have advantage of a wealth of tools and materials for this task, developed over ages by scholars and rabbis."

He went on from there in his dusty mellifluous voice, saying nothing profound or original, even nothing so much as sincere and true. Until the last five minutes his approval rating must have been 100 percent. Who could disagree? Then without a pause he shifted to a new theme.

"What separates conventional from prophetic education is process of abstraction applied to life. Life, history, social development does not repeat itself and who repeats patterns of yesterday is soon out of step, both with life and with matrix of their own knowledge. Being true to values in changing world requires continual reinterpretation, reapplication. Now that may be disquieting to some for it means doing things differently and some people find security in repetition. But life is not search for security. It is process of adaptation."

He stopped talking and looked at us, seeking confirmation. A few of the Board members seemed uncomfortable. Finkelstein was clearing his throat and running his hand through his unruly red hair, signs of agitation.

"Some of you may be surprised," Lev continued, walking a few steps toward the edge of the stage. "Some may be disturbed by what this school will become. But in end you will not regret result. Here, we will try to kindle light unto nations by dedication to universal justice and compassion and understanding." Again, he gazed around the group while the abstraction sunk in. I could feel the release of tension. After all, who could disagree? But the relief was premature.

"And to that end," said Lev, his voice now a little louder, "to that end, Sami Arakat has been admitted into eighth form. I have interviewed him, reviewed his records and find him to be a fine young man with a bright inquisitive mind."

A chorus of inhaled breath was the response. I looked around me and saw surprise, even mild indignation. Everybody knew Sami. A nice boy, he was the oldest son of Mumzer and Mary Arakat, Bolton's Palestinian grocer. But to admit him to the first class of the Jewish day school, without a word of consultation with the Board, was rash.

He stopped and waited for a moment, this time looking into our faces with inquiry, as if he were trying to measure our reaction to the news. There was silence then a single, frail clapping began against the wall. It was Selma Novik, soon joined by the others, more polite than enthusiastic.

# NINE

# Daily Bread

L et's face it, everybody is in love with their own opinions. And on the same subject the most open-minded human being is a hypocrite. At heart he is contemptuous of ideas that fall too far from the tree of his own special knowledge. So it didn't surprise me at all that the Board left the reception muttering to each other, "What made him do that?" At this point they were too polite to confront Lev Kyol. Besides, he was a stranger to our customs. You don't tell a person without shoes to leave his galoshes in the hall, after all.

Understand: the Board members had their opinions about Palestinian rights, the PLO, and all that. Palestinians were people and if they could live peacefully with the Israelis (although most doubted that they could) they should be able to live in peace and not be bothered. And that had nothing to do with the Arakat family. They don't throw stones. They are a nice, decent family working long hours in a store to get ahead so that someday they could buy the building, put their kids through

Penn State, see them married and move to Phoenix. In short, they shared the American dream with everybody else.

At least that's what Finkelstein said as we were leaving the building. He said it in a quizzical, apologetic tone and he even took my elbow as if to help me agree with him.

"Mendel, tell me, is it right, even if we don't have a lot of students yet...is it right to introduce Christians, or Muslims into a Jewish school? Why...why would they want to be there?" He opened both of his palms in the traditional gesture of "who knows?" and scrunched up his face.

"Don't sell short, Finkelstein," I said. "Maybe Arakat just wants his boy to have a pluralistic education. Maybe he thinks the public schools are no good, the same as Nudelman."

"But there's the Christian Fellowship School."

"Maybe that's too parochial. Maybe he thinks he'll get a better education. I don't know. Why don't you ask him? Or ask the director." I stepped aside to let Rosenzweig and Harriet pass, as we had stopped in our tracks to finish the discussion.

"You're right Mendel. Let's ask him."

"Finkelstein, for me it's not a question. If you want my opinion, I think it's great. You ask him."

"Mendel, I don't know him. You, on the other hand, are our true ecumenicist. You know him."

"What's ecumenical about liking falafel and dolma. They've got great carryout."

"So let's both ask him. I've never had a falafel. How about lunch tomorrow?" said Finkelstein.

"You buy."

Arakat's All Purpose occupied the bottom story of a dirty brick building within sight, sound, and smell of the steelworks. Across the street, the polished grey strands of the railroad tracks mated and were swallowed by the wide toothless mouth of a long, corrugated building that, by the sound of what was happening inside, had a chronic case of industrial indigestion. The location was a good one. Just across Second Street was Sam's Bar and Grill, a popular watering spot for the mill workers because of Sam's check-cashing policy and his two-drinks-for-ninety-nine-cents special on payday.

Arakat's All Purpose had once been a general store owned by the Horowitz clan, who long ago had given up retailing for real estate and now owned a seven-story office building in Pittsburgh, free and clear.

Inside was everything you needed. According to the faded sign over the counter, If we don't have it, you don't need it. The room was warmly lit by hanging globes, the light reflecting off of the greasy yellow pressed-tin ceiling. The floor was cracked asbestos tile, green and cream. A long deli case was sweating, the two rows of grocery racks had everything the A&P had, only fewer, and for a little bit more money, since Arakat had to pay more too. The smell was like every small store you've ever been in, a mixture of laundry detergent, chilling vegetables, potato salad, ham, and gum balls—you could fill up on the smell. Arakat's store was comforting, unchanging, nurturing and nostalgic.

There was a line at the deli counter; three high school kids buying lunch and thumbing through *Seventeen* or *People* while they waited. Mumzer Arakat was smiling at the register,

ringing up the order of a pasty-faced woman wearing a bulging yellow floral dress. A hard way to make a buck, I thought.
Three cents' profit here, a nickel there, but no matter how bad
it gets people have to eat. He saw me and acknowledged me
with a wider smile, between ringing up a can of chili and a loaf
of spongy bread.

Mumzer Arakat is somebody I like. He is just plain nice.
If he came to the synagogue he would blend right in with his
round, black, sensitive eyes and a nose that droops a little, not
to mention the worry lines on his forehead. Mary is stout and
has frizzy red hair. She would fit in as well. I've never been to
their house but I've chewed the fat with them during the lulls
in their business.

Finkelstein was looking a little like we had just crossed
the Green Line into the West Bank—his smile was rigid and
formal.

"And what else, Mrs. Ridzinski?" While he took her money
he asked her about her bronchitis and whether her aunt had
gone back to Beaver Falls.

To me he said, "Falafel?" I never ate anything else.

"Two."

Although Mary was no more than a few feet away, Mumzer
called out, "Two falafel," and she replied, "Coming up." It was
a ritual with them, something they had picked up in a diner
their first week in America. It was, for them, the American way.
Mary went on with the quick layering of a turkey sandwich on
whole wheat for one of the kids.

I introduced Finkelstein and saw a glint of bemused curiosity in Arakat's eyes as he offered his hand across the counter

and shifted from one foot to the other. His feet must get tired standing as he does all day.

"You heard about Sami?" Arakat said.

"Yes.

"Now that you mention it, Mumzer, you've got people wondering why?"

"Why not?"

Finkelstein raised his hands. "Only Jews answer a question with another question."

"You have a monopoly?" asked Mumzer.

"Of course he is welcome!" Finkelstein cleared his throat like a revving motorcycle, a sure sign he was uncomfortable.

"So the director said. He's a sympathetic man, this Mr. Kyol." Mumzer drummed on the worn grey linoleum of the counter and looked around the store scanning, no doubt, for shoplifters. His eyes finally landed amiably on Finkelstein.

"To answer your question, Mary and I thought about it a lot. There must be something to Jewish education and values, we figured, to have produced so many brilliant scientists. Einstein—"

"I think he went to public school," said Finkelstein.

Mumzer looked at Finkelstein with a question. "Are you trying to tell me something, Mr. Finkelstein: should I read between the lines?"

"No, Mumzer, he's just curious."

"Listen, I'll confess something." Mumzer leaned on his elbow and his voice took on a confidential, smiling tone. "Sami's best friend is Isaac Nudelman. There you have most of the reason; that and the belief that he'd get a better education.

Every time you pick up the paper you read of budget cuts in this and that, the schools and the police and so on."

A strand of understanding bound Mumzer and Finkelstein at that moment.

"You want some coffee? It's a fresh pot," said Mumzer, his hand on the plastic wrap-covered keys of the register. "The drinks are on me."

Mary handed each of us a falafel wrapped at one end in white paper.

"How do you eat this?" said Finkelstein, reaching for a napkin and looking apprehensively at the open mouth of the pita bread stuffed with crisp brown balls of fried garbanzo paste, lettuce, tomato, and hummus sauce. "It looks like it wants to eat me."

We gobbled the falafel and drank the coffee, kibitzing all the while with Mary and Mumzer about the coming election, the coming football season, and Mumzer's uncle who had just died of cancer at the age of 87.

Back outside in the din of the mill and the hazy afternoon sunlight, I said, "So what do you think now?"

"Thanks."

"For what? You paid."

"You know what for." And I did.

We walked back to the car and suddenly Finkelstein chuckled to himself and said, "Do you think Arakat has any idea that *mumzer* means "bastard" in Hebrew?"

"Ask him."

## TEN

# On Forgiving Debts

<hr>

R osenzweig leaned toward me and squinted confidentially as if he was about to make a momentous announcement, one that would change my life, as in fact it did. "Mendel, we've decided that you should serve as official liaison between the school and the synagogue."

"I'm flattered by the honor, but I couldn't do it justice." I wasn't flattered at all, but it would be interesting.

"I know it's a burden, Mendel," said Nudelman. "You have more than your share already." He looked from me to the two boys laboring toward the entrance of the building with a black trunk between them.

"You've already won the director's confidence. He trusts you," Rosenzweig wheedled, toying with his unlit cigar.

"Only because I supported the admission of Sami Arakat," I said, thinking of the inquiry of the Board and the expressions of surprise from the community. Quite a little snit had developed, with at least four different points of view. Not to mention the tender of resignation of one of the teachers, Norman

Bron, who, we found out, believed that Palestinians should be offered one-way tickets to Amman. Nudelman had talked him into staying.

"More than that. You get along with everybody. It's your nature," Nudelman added.

Funny how a person gets a reputation for something based upon as little as a single incident. Back in high school, during my tenure as assistant manager of the basketball team, the Bolton Bulls, I had gotten two enemies, competitors for the same position, to shake hands and actually stop calling each other insulting ethnic names. One was Polish, the other Hungarian. Since that time I'd been a candidate for the Nobel Peace Prize in Nudelman's mind.

"Lev Kyol can take care of himself and the school. He's tough and sensible, too," I said feeling like a tennis ball before the tournament. "Not that I won't help."

"Think of it as helping Lev, Mendel. He's a complete stranger, a refugee." Now he was tugging at my guts. Nudelman did know how to get to people.

We all stopped to watch two boys fielding fly balls. The ball arced high, suspended for a moment in the air, uncertain what to do, then fell. Mitt pointed up, and one of the boys danced back and forth until he was just under the ball. It slapped into his mitt, he stepped back and snapped the ball back into the air. The other boy ran backwards just missing Gene Karp, who was shambling down the path, his head bent into a newspaper. Karp looked up with a startled scowl as the boy ran past.

"You see how it is, Mendel? The tolerances are still pretty fine all around," said Nudelman.

"Have they chosen school colors?" asked Rosenzweig.

They were always doing something like this, at the last moment. Here we were on the way to a meeting with the faculty and no doubt they wanted to announce my so-called honor without giving me so much as a night to think it over. Not that I could say no; they knew that. I never said no, it wasn't in my vocabulary.

"Think of the excitement, Mendel, being an intimate part of the school the first year," Nudelman said, of course.

"Travel, adventure. You sound like an army recruiting sergeant," I said.

"I knew we could count on you," said Rosenzweig. "Now, let me share another problem, not that it's anything you can't handle, but you should know all the same." He and Nudelman exchanged apprehensive looks.

"We want your opinion, Mendel, on whether we should tell Kyol about it at this time."

"Stop beating the bush around," I said. "We have two minutes till ground zero."

"Read it for yourself," said Rosenzweig, breathless with anxiety. We weren't going up hill.

He handed me a letter with a lawyers' letterhead—black and shiny, and embossed like the back of a cockroach—with a Pittsburgh address, and signed Duckhorn, Pittler & Still. It was from the living members of the Mossberg family. They had heard about the transformation of the old people's home into a school and wanted the endowment back, the whole six million dollars. The lawyers weren't that direct, but that's what it said. My heart sank a little, but somehow, I wasn't troubled. After all, the old folks were happy. The money had been there so long and wasn't being put to any use.

"So, Mendel?"

"Don't tell him, not now at least. He's got enough on his mind," I said, and that was my first deception, one I still regret.

Nudelman nodded. "My feelings exactly. Rosenzweig will answer and my guess is they will be satisfied."

"So, let's go in."

# ELEVEN

# Equal Treatment

---

Over the next month or so order and chaos were room-mates. School started and the building took on a different sound and look. Classroom walls filled with posters of Jerusalem, Einstein, and Martin Luther King. New green chalkboards were decorated with the graffiti of learning: words, Hebrew letters, algebraic formulae, historical date lines, and provocative questions. The halls would go from echoing stillness to raucous laughter, thumping, dragging feet, and exuberant, youthful shouts. After class the lawn sounded with the referee's whistle, the thunk of a soccer ball against a forehead and the animal shouts of disappointment and triumph.

As for chaos (for that was order), there was the struggle of eight teachers and the director to know each other's limits, predict each other's failings and strengths, to move from a room full of strangers to some sort of collegiality, to work more together than against each other.

They were so different, these eight. Cohan was not Jewish, but an extroverted Irish humanist and Universalist. In contrast,

Schweig was closed and parochial. He resented the admission of Sami Arakat and let it be known. Between these two were all shades of character, attitude, and opinion.

The same with the students. Drawn from all over the country, except for our town kids, they came from either rich homes or broken homes. Some homes were both rich and broken. No sooner had they unpacked than groups began to form—groups of inclusion and exclusion, They formed little tribes with their own likes and dislikes, their own hangouts (the cavernous attic or the hay loft), and their own interests (soccer, computer games). One boy even was a bird watcher, which made Selma happy.

As for the Mossberg Trust and the letter from the Pittsburgh attorney, nobody, except for Rosenzweig, gave it much thought. As he put it, we had just revitalized it. The Board simply clucked its collective tongue and dispatched a pusillanimous letter from Rosenzweig to the attorneys for the family. With that they turned their collective backs on it with all the denial of an early cancer patient.

If the Board wanted to pretend that, like the national debt, the problem would somehow go away, I didn't share their nearsighted view and neither did Nudelman. He had Rosenzweig hire an investigator to find out what he could about the Mossberg family. Rosenzweig liked the idea. Hardly anybody remembered the Mossbergs as they had packed up and moved to Los Angeles in 1947.

I had my own investigator/historian, Selma Novik. She remembered. Moses Mossberg had set up the endowment for the old- folks home while Mossberg's was still the largest department store in Monogenessen County. According to

Selma, Moses's great uncle had died on the street, homeless, in Lvov, my hometown. Moses's two sons, Morris and Casper, sold the store after the old man passed away and invested the boodle in something called the Miracle Mile. Selma had no idea what that was, but it sounded good.

"Casper wrote to me once," she said, her eyes looking into the past, "and I answered, but I never heard from him again. California was a long way from Bolton in those days." Talking about travel she began to describe a train trip she had taken to Chicago to attend her niece's wedding in 1947. So much for the trust. More later.

Beyond the normal break-in troubles was a growing discomfort with Lev Kyol's eccentric and individualistic leadership. The flap over the admission of Sami Arakat passed, but it left a residue of doubt. Some, initially bothered like Finkelstein, came to favor it.

People don't like change until it's old hat. Later they accept it without question, defend it as a sacred right, even if it's poisoning them. Take coffee and cigarettes. You have no idea the ruckus they created when they were first introduced to the world. There I go again.

Lev added cayenne pepper to many dinner conversations and extended Heda Finkelstein's telephone calls until even Finkelstein complained that he could never get through to her. Of course the raised eyebrows and twitches of the community were not universal. Like a good sauce, or reality, it was hard to break his performance down into parts, let alone say what he was doing right or wrong. But let me try.

Lev's leadership was authoritarian democracy, which is to say that he insisted on a full discussion of everything, so long as he had the last word. This didn't endear him to the teachers, for if they were to spend time in meetings when they could be grading papers they wanted something to show for it. He was brilliant, but it was an unfamiliar brilliance, brilliance with a Slavic accent. He was personable, magnetic, when you were with him, but at the same time remote, otherworldly. Then there were these gestures: theatrical or substantive. No one was sure.

For example, as soon the community digested the admission of Sami Arakat, Lev raised another fuss with a daily morning prayer and flag raising, in all weather, out in front of the school. Several parents complained, having heard about it from their runny-nosed children.

I got called, and off I went for a "routine investigation," feeling like a cop. Rather than talk about it in the abstract, I drove out on a late autumn morning to take in the ceremony. It had rained and the bruised clouds filled the sky and spilled over the rolling horizon. Tree limbs were lacquered with the rain and faded leaves clung desperately to the nearly naked branches. The wind from the storm was tired and fitful, chilling as a cold shower. I got stuck behind a slow-moving truck filled with dirt and almost missed the ceremony.

Slipping on the wet brick of the path, I hurried toward the circle of children and teachers, relieved to see that they were still dressed in their jackets and raincoats at least. the Stars and Stripes was already at the top of the aluminum painted pole and alternately crackling and falling limp in the fluky breeze.

Gathered in a circle around the pole, the children were chanting a morning prayer. Isaac Nudelman, wearing a red sweater was standing between Sami and Suzy Roe. Suzy's fine blond hair kept blowing over her eyes and she had her hand up to push it back. Sami's lips weren't moving.

Next came the school oath, another innovation in which a child pledged to do the best he could in every endeavor. They started with one boy and each one repeated a phrase of it until they came around the circle. "Don't hold back from any task, concentrate, be considerate of others, perform an act of public service each week and a good deed each day," and a few other thoughts equally beneficial. After a moment of silence, and a few announcements by the wire-haired Mr. Shusterman about "try outs" for a play, the circle broke into twos and threes and made for the double door of the grey stone building.

Unnoticed, I waited until everyone was inside before searching out Lev's office, the sitting room of his small apartment on the second floor. The halls were in good order, the wood polished and smelling of pine cleanser. On my way I peeked into two of the classrooms at students taking their seats with varying degrees of interest and indifference.

With its dark oak paneling and grey stone fireplace with a Tudor peak, Lev's office looked like the study of a down-at-the-heels country squire. Most of the floor was covered up to the edge of the radiator with a flat green carpet faded to the hue of dead moss. His desk was mahogany and covered with a thick piece of glass that reflected green on the edges.

He stood as I entered and his wooden swivel chair pitched drunkenly and shuddered. He walked around the desk and opened his arms to greet me with an abstract embrace. He was as shabby as the carpet. His pants were mouse grey, bagged at the knee and too short so that wrinkled socks could be seen above the cracked surface of his heavy shoes. The cardigan that he usually wore had once been a feast for moths and was surgically stitched here and there.

"Mendel, my dear," he said in that smoky, soft voice. I always waited for him to finish—dear what? But he never did. I'm not the one to talk about English misplaced. "So good for you to come. Sit, please. We have many things to talk over. First, some tea."

I sat down in the brittle and cracked leather armchair and watched him fuss with the tea; the kettle was already exhaling steam on its hot plate. He put two spoonfuls of black smoky Russian tea in an aluminum-perforated canister, and so on. We all know about a Russian and his tea.

"I had samovar in Moskva, but I couldn't take it to America, you see." Without asking, he put several sugar cubes on the saucer and a tea cake that had the signature of Selma Novik. "Selma is making me fat with her cakes."

"You are well taken care of here," I said.

"Yes, people kind to me. You know, Estelle Cantor, what's the word, straightened…no, ironed my shirts. She said I make bad impression with wrinkled shirts." He touched his heart and his head with his finger. "It's what's here and here that matters, Mendel, do you agree? And what you say and do."

So Estelle was still taking care of him. I couldn't help feeling a stitch of envy and regret that I hadn't somehow let her know that I too would welcome more than a meal and a cup of coffee. "You do look," I paused searching for a word that wouldn't be too offensive. "You look like a professor."

He sat down on the edge of his desk, leaned back on his hands and nickered like a horse, a soft laugh that came from someplace deep in his chest and went well with his long equine face. "So Mendel, we have business. Who shall start first? You or me?"

"Yes, so I'll begin." I balanced my teacup on the round arm of the chair and spoke. "The Board wanted me to tell you about a problem that shouldn't concern you but could affect the fate of the school."

The strand of graying hair that crossed his largely bare scalp slid over the furrows of his forehead and he pushed it back and gave me his attention.

I slowly explained the history of the school leading up to the letter from the attorneys. He was still gazing at me from his perch, looking a little disinterested. "To make a long story longer, Rosenzweig wrote a nice letter telling them they were wrong, which they didn't buy. Their answer is a suit to take the property back, not to mention the six- million- dollar endowment. They want to tear down the buildings and build a high tech industrial park or something like that." I heard my voice go limp as I finished. Nobody likes to be the bearer of bad news.

He took a deep breath and pitched a little forward before he got up and poured some more tea for himself. If the news troubled him he didn't exactly show it, although I thought he went paler than usual. I waited as he stirred three cubes of sugar into his tea.

"Waste of paper to wrap each cube," he finally said.

"Americans are very sanitary."

"So thank you, Mendel. I suppose we should tell teachers, parents that what, this could be last year? How much time do we have?"

"Look, Lev, it's not over yet. It's just starting. We may win the case, or it could drag on for years."

"Yes, I have read Dickens, *Bleak House*. It could drag on."

"At this point, the Board sees no reason to alarm people. But there is a hearing coming up in a few weeks. A temporary injunction or something. Don't ask me to explain."

"Mendel, you do not need to. It is not in my power. I will focus on school. It will survive. I need very little."

"Your needs are not the issue, Lev. The school costs a lot of money to operate."

"We will find a way. Listen, on that subject, we are going to have a dinner to raise some money."

"Have you talked to anybody on the Board?"

"I am telling you."

"So tell, I'm all ears." He had dismissed the first great crisis as if it were no more than a broken window. What equanimity. Is it the mark of a great leader to stay cool when others are spinning with fear or was he just foolish?

He looked suddenly enthusiastic as he said, "It will be dinner for homeless to raise money for St. Ambrose shelter."

"St. Ambrose, the patron saint of Jewish day schools." I couldn't resist the sarcasm.

"Was he? But you jest." (Nobody says that. It must have come from reading Dickens)

"Isn't that a little off the mark? Do you, does anybody, have time for this in the first few months of the school's history?"

"It is educational. All students are participating. They will cook and serve and sell tickets. It is already planned. Even down to menu and cost."

"Menus are a serious business here in Bolton, Lev. You need guidance." My irritation with him was vibrating through my body but I did my best to hide it. "You want to start off on the right foot."

"No, it is Russian menu, just right."

"Something your mother used to make."

"Not exactly. Kasha. Gruel, you call it." (Again Dickens)

"Interesting." I had never had high blood- pressure but I could feel it coming on. "And the next course?"

"That is it. A few grams of kasha with a dollop of chicken fat. Hot water, a little stale black bread."

"I see." I finally got the point. It was bold and original, but would people sit for it? The idea spread like ice down my back. It was suicide; to serve kasha and give the dinner proceeds to a Catholic hostel when the school needed direct support. He was going too far. All the same, I had to admire him for it.

"What do you think, Mendel?" He was leaning against his desk bent toward me, his expression both earnest and innocent.

"What do I think? I'll tell you what I think. It's risky. On top of your admission of a Palestinian they'll think you're off your trolley." For a moment he didn't understand then he smiled at the expression. "How is Sami doing by the way?" I asked eager to change the subject.

"He's fine, I think. He has some students, not all, interested in Palestinian people. That is what I wanted next to tell you. We are having Palestine National Day. There will be music, a flag and Liam Cohan is giving a lecture. He's Irish you know, an Irish nationalist; a fascinating man. He despises British."

The words went down like uncooked matzo balls. Palestinian flags. Jews who turned out to be Irish. I must confess I wanted to laugh, but all the same, I cringed at the thought of the Board's reaction. This was, after all a Jewish school and the Board wasn't exactly visionary.

I stood and walked around the desk. "Lev," I said, my tone one of sincere concern. "I think you go a little too far too fast."

He turned his head toward me with a look of fuddled discomfort. "This is not Soviet Union, Mendel. Education is not just scratch with chalk on blackboard or chapter 14 read tonight, test tomorrow. It is doing, feeling, seeing, total; not just kids, but parents too."

"But," I looked for a way of saying it, "too many new ideas are indigestible; they get thrown back."

"This is so little, Mendel." He looked as though I had opened a trap door under him.

What could I say to that look? "You want me to tell the Board all this."

"It is your job, Mendel."

"I'll do my best," I said, feeling like the lawyer representing an inmate on death row.

I patted him on the shoulder, shook his hand and left the room with a thank you for the tea.

Once in the hall I breathed the school disinfectant smell as though it were roses. Given the lawsuit, Lev's erratic brilliance would turn the Board on its head. Of this I was sure. I agreed in principle with everything he was doing but I was only the messenger and principle wasn't always possible in this world.

I passed the day room where faculty and the old folks passed the time together. With its crackled leather sofa and cast-off arm-chairs it had the look of a rescue mission except for the vase of late marigolds on the scored oak library table along with the disorder of *Atlantic Monthly*, *Hadassah*, *Time*, and *Jerusalem Post* strewn among the white tea pot and random mugs.

Izzy Bortz and Gene Karp were in the corner muttering over a game of cards. Selma Novik was seated in silhouette next to the wide mullioned window, which looked out on the lawn and embraced the fanning limbs of a chestnut tree. I hesitated at the door, unsure whether I could absorb another word, but she saw me and beckoned. The air was close. Tobacco smoke competed with the lemon spice of the roses.

I sat down with unease on an unstable chair with a wicker seat. The light from the window seemed to pass through Selma; she might have been carved out of alabaster. She put her knitting on the table beside her, folded her thin hands on her lap and focused her eyes on me.

"Mendel, how nice to see you. Help yourself to some tea. I just made it."

"I've just had some."

"Then you've been visiting Lev. He drinks more than all of us put together," she said, looking as though she had disclosed a secret vice.

"So how are things," I asked, chiding myself for seeking information instead of just being social, and above all recognizing the irony in my question.

"It's grand, Mendel, just grand. Having these children around us, even with all the clamor, has given us all a new lease on life. Even the grumps." She pointed a finger at Bortz and Karp. "Our lives are so full now." Her eye drifted away from mine, and I thought she'd lost her train of thought as she looked toward the crown of the tree. "I think that's a tanager up there near the top, can you see it?"

"I wouldn't know, Selma."

I looked over her thin shoulder and saw Maimonides Kravitz, pruning shears in hand, about to prune a rose bush. Next to him, as attentive as young birds waiting to be fed, were two young boys. Mi was nodding, gesturing at the thorny branch, and then pointing down at the roots, lecturing them on horticulture, and the students, at least one of them, looked interested. Kravitz bent low to remove a dead leaf from the carefully mulched soil and his many-colored *keepah* dropped to the ground. The smallest boy picked it up and handed it to him. That told me all I needed to know.

## TWELVE

# What a Candle Knows

Putting the school behind me I beat a trail to Estelle's house. I wanted to unburden myself and she was the only one who would hear me and offer level-headed advice. There was yet another reason: jealousy, the termite, was gnawing at my trust. She was ironing his shirts, treating him like her child or what else. I know myself, even though the mirror in which I see my image has lost some of its silver. I tossed the jealousy out the window of the car like an apple core only to find it back again. Still, recognizing it, I could deal with it, or so I thought.

Enough self-abuse. I found Estelle at the dining room table bent over the *Wall Street Journal*, squinting through her half-lens reading glasses at those mystical, hieratic columns that represent to her and others the formula that turns paper into gold, the stock listings. She was still investing and beating Mr. Dow and Mr. Jones, whoever they might be.

I let myself in with my personal key and with the wall-to-wall and my soft soles she hadn't even heard me. I cleared my throat and she jumped as though she'd been shocked, before looking at me over the rim of her glasses with apologetic irritation.

"You startled me, Mendel!"

"You'll go blind reading that gibberish."

"My broker told me to sell H. J. Heinz."

"I've always preferred Campbell's myself."

She stood and walked toward me, her slightly full figure rolling under the red silk of her dress. "Mendel!" She shook her head, gave me a bemused critical look and touched her lips to my cheek. "Come in the kitchen. I'll make you some tea and warm up some cinnamon bread."

I followed her and sat down at the maple table. While she put the tea together, we chatted about this and that. Heda Finkelstein's fear that she had cancer had been downgraded to a possible spastic esophagus. Steve White had gotten into an intersection accident and the man who hit him had brandished a pistol when Steve asked him for his insurance. Sarah Nudelman won a trip to Disneyland in a Betty Crocker contest. Just the usual.

I held back my own news, fairly choking on it until she was seated, and the fragrance of the toasted cinnamon bread had finally overcome the smell of chicken stock simmering on the stove. Even though she lived alone, there was always something cooking. Who was the soup for, Lev perhaps? My jealousy was like Heda's spastic esophagus!

Avoiding any mention of her relationship with Lev, I told her about the St. Anthony (or was it Ambrose) kasha party.

She wrinkled her face distastefully at that and said, "Do you think he has a good recipe? I'm only kidding."

"I'm not laughing. He's committing pedagogical suicide."

"Mendel, at least he's true to his convictions."

"But life involves compromise."

"So, what would be more acceptable to the Board? A dinner to aid the Jewish homeless?" She twisted her lips to one side and squinted at me.

"If it were only that," I said, and I told her about the planned celebration of Palestine Day. Her eyebrows lifted, and her breath caught at that. I finished with the good stuff, the interplay between the old and the young, so that she would have a balanced view.

"Yes," she said.

"I'm afraid to tell the Board about this. They will trade poor Lev for a case of Stolichnaya when they hear." She answered with a sober assenting nod. "You know him as well as I do, if not better. You have his ear. Reason with him."

"He's not afraid of the consequences of what he does, Mendel. He wants to be true to himself."

"You already said that." A secret was written in her troubled look. She knew something. "What?" I asked. "You know something you're not saying."

"Mendel, if you told me something, you wouldn't want me to break your confidence, would you?" Her voice was soft but stubborn and I knew Estelle. No amount of persuasion would pry the secret out of her.

"What do we do?" I raised my hands and fluttered my fingers.

"So, it's we, is it?"

"Yes. You have as much responsibility for him as I do."

Estelle reached back and arranged her hair. She stared out the window at the red leafed plum in the center of the yard, possibly remembering the day it was planted. I waited.

"As for the dinner," she finally said, completing a thought, "you just tell the Board that Lev wants to get the non-Jewish community to support the school. He wants to raise money that way. They'll understand that."

"Maybe they will. I doubt that Nudelman will buy it. Is there any truth to it?"

"Who knows? But it's something they can believe and accept."

"What about the food?"

"I'll handle that. Don't even mention it." She had come through in a pinch. She always did. I remembered how she had saved Sydney from ruin with her little nest egg. Estelle should be President.

"And how about Palestine Day?"

"Mendel, you'll think of something." She stood up looking gently impatient. "If the taste of pepper is too strong, throw in some other spices. That's what my mother told me."

"Estelle, you are brilliant. Just one more question."

"What?"

"Why are you ironing his shirts?"

"Have you seen him?"

# THIRTEEN

# Swallow A Cow

That evening, my rhetorical strategy in order, I went to see Nudelman. I found him on the apron of his two-car garage, giving Mandalay, his venerable Labrador, a bath. Maybe the dog was giving him a shower, for I wasn't sure which of them was more soaked. Nudelman's baggy khaki pants and his smoky green plaid shirt were stuck to his body. The dog, usually solemn, was jumping, springing, and animated as Nudelman showered him with the garden hose. Mandalay ran at it, tried to bite the stream of water, blinked and lumbered toward me with the obvious notion of including me in the fun. Before I could back away, he had begun one of those sequential shakes that dogs do, beginning at the head, making his jowls rattle against his yellow teeth, proceeding to the hulk of his body, his long black hair dancing, and finally switching his tail. Not sure of the result, he stood up and put both lumpy wet paws on my chest as if to inspect his work.

"Mandy!" said Nudelman a little late, and the dog dropped to the ground and bounded toward the hose. "Sorry, Mendel," said Nudelman as he squeezed the hose nozzle to a trickle.

Nudelman had always had a Labrador retriever, one after another, since high school, even though he never went hunting. The poor dogs grew up believing that old tennis shoes were ducks.

I went to his cluttered study and waited while he changed clothes. There was, as usual, no place to sit. When we were in high school and I visited his bed room I would always sit on the floor. Removing the glossy brochures advertising GM long haul tractors from the seat of the black lacquer chair with the Penn State seal on the back, I sat down and looked across the surface of his desk at a fan of legal looking papers. Reading them upside down I gathered that Nudelman was buying a truck dealership in Slippery Rock. Where did he get the energy? Where did he get the money?

"My father is buying another dealership." It was Isaac's voice, matter of fact, precise even for a thirteen-year old, every noun and consonant in its place. I turned and looked at him, a small model of his father with the same unmanageable bush of black hair and all-knowing hound's eyes. Maybe Nudelman kept getting Labradors because they looked like him.

"I was just about to use the computer," Isaac said, going to the table against the wall on which sat a cyclopean Macintosh, its silicon mind even now digesting what looked like the last five years of profits of Nudelman's truck dealership. By the sound of its contented hum, business had been good.

Isaac sat down and began to punch the keys, making the computer swallow the profits and regurgitate what looked like a labyrinth peopled by frenetic little block people that exploded with the sound of an electronic blowout.

"How's school, Isaac?"

"What?" His voice came from another planet. "Oh. Fine."

"Tell me, how's Sami doing? Is Mr. Schweig treating him fairly?"

Isaac turned to look at me, not directly, for kids his age, tend to look around and through adults. "Why?"

"I just wondered. I know he thinks Palestinians ought to move to Jordan."

"He's OK."

"What teachers do you like particularly?"

"Mr. Shusterman's nice. So is Miss Karman." Isaac, by the look of him, had said all he was going to say.

"Not interested in computer games, Mendel?" said Nudelman, now wearing dry brown corduroy pants and green and blue plaid shirt.

"It's like Japanese to me."

"Excuse me, Mendel. Homework." Isaac darted out of the room like a broken- field runner.

"We've just installed a LAN at the shop," said Nudelman following his son with a father's eyes. "All the parts inventory at your fingertips. Even in my office. Soon we'll be able to order parts just by pushing a few buttons on the keyboard, like the ATM."

"I don't have an ATM card, Nudelman."

Nudelman looked at me as if I had told him that tomorrow the earth would be destroyed by a giant meteor. Then he shook his head indulgently and patted my shoulder. "Maybe you're better off. But you didn't come here to talk about that."

He pulled a pipe out of his volcanic ashtray and began to stuff it with tobacco. It smelled so rich coming out of the jar that I wondered why he wanted to burn it.

"Where's Sarah?" I asked, putting off the message as long as I could.

"Visiting her mother." Sarah's mother lived on the air-conditioned twenty-fourth floor of a condo in some anonymous town in Florida, one of those places where the shopping mall parking lot is full of golf carts, according to Nudelman, who had gone there once.

"I wanted to give you the news from the school in advance of the Board meeting."

"Good. I haven't heard from Lev in a while. He doesn't like the telephone, it seems." His husky voice dropped with a hint of disapproval. "And I've been so damned busy. I've just bought a dealership in McKeesport. Wanna go into the truck business, Mendel? I need somebody I can trust out there."

"Nudelman, have I ever remotely resembled a businessman."

"Only kidding. So, what's up? You look like you've got something on your mind."

I couldn't put it off. Gilding the news as best I could I told him about the dinner and gave him time to digest it. He shrugged.

"Who can disagree with a dinner to help the homeless?"

Next, I hit him with the nationalities- day—that's how I put it.

"What's this nationalities day?" His worry lines were an inch deep.

"The stateless people of the world, the Kurds, the Sudanese Christians, the Palestinians."

"I thought you were building up to that." He waved his pipe idly and drew in his lips. Don't misunderstand. He was sympathetic to the Palestinian cause as long as it didn't take anything away from the Jews, but as a GM truck dealer he wasn't going to put the new Ford line on display in his showroom.

"Jesus," he muttered with an ironic smile before he plugged his pipe into it. "Mendel, can you get him to tone it down? Even better, put it on ice. Put it off till next year."

"He marches to his own flute."

"You mean drum."

"Whatever, you get the meaning."

He looked across the room at the little gold-plated basketball player on its black plastic pedestal. I followed his eyes.

"Remember how simple life was then?" he said.

Simple for him maybe. Not for me.

# FOURTEEN

# What to Do With The Right Eye

Given a choice between the extraction of a wisdom tooth and going to the Board meeting, I'm not sure which I would have preferred. In making that statement, I'm telling you something about myself, as if you don't already know it. Why should I worry about what happens, I'm not the director, I'm not being paid to be the liaison, and I'm not on the Board. My life and the world will go on whatever happens. Speeding tickets will be given out, mothers will buy their children shoes that are too big, in short, and life will hardly change. But I am like that tribe of Indians who think that if they don't get up at dawn and welcome the sun, it won't pay us a visit. Ethnocentricity, narcissism, whatever, it would be nice not to care, but I do.

There I was in the boardroom of the school, hospitably pouring coffee into those old china mugs, and there they all were, seated around the long table. Rabbi Bing was looking blind as he polished his thick crystalline glasses. Nudelman was pushing his hair back and smiling at some pleasant recollection. Finkelstein was looking sidelong at the sports page. There were others in the room, as well: Mi Kravitz, representing the old folks and two teachers, ominous in that they had the reputation of disagreeing on almost everything. One of them, Menachem Harney, was a pugnacious-looking Israeli who had refused to serve in the Israeli Army. The other, Schweig, whose close-set eyes seemed to touch, had never been in any army by the look of him, but he supported unlimited Jewish settlement of the West Bank. There were others but I'm not the secretary after all.

Nudelman looked at his watch, chewed on the corner of his mouth and rapped the ashtray on the tabletop to call the meeting to order. He had been waiting for Rosenzweig, who was due back from court. This was the big day; the hearing on the case that had been filed by the heirs of the Mossberg family. They were trying to get what Rosenzweig called a preliminary injunction, tying up the endowment that was now being used to offset the deficit of the school.

Just saying the words "preliminary injunction" gave me heartburn but Rosenzweig talked a good confidence game, as they say. There was the "status quo" on our side, which didn't sound very Jewish, not to mention the "equities" and a lack of "irreparable injury"—he had personally researched the matter. Besides, Judge McGorty, the jurist hearing the case, was a fellow Mason, and a member of his poker club, while the Mossberg attorneys were a "pin striped crowd out of Pittsburgh who looked down their noses at any courthouse that had windows that opened" and so on.

Despite all of this, Nudelman looked a little nervous, at least until Lev Kyol shambled into the room, an amber glass of tea held in front of him like a communion cup. He set the glass down next to Nudelman, slopping a little on the tabletop, shook Nudelman's hand, and with a sweeping good-hearted nod to the rest of us said, "So let's begin."

Begin we did! "What is this Palestinian celebration?", "Aren't the Macabees good enough?" "Comfort to the enemy?" and so on from Finkelstein, who was always something of a complainer despite his good heart.

Lev just looked at him with an expression that was both understanding and forgiving.

"Education is not all sugar."

"Please, I'm talking practicality. I don't need parables." Finkelstein pressed on. "You want a saying? Don't give succor to the enemy."

"We have no enemies but ourselves," said Lev, sounding like a patient teacher speaking to a slow learner.

"So, what were the Nazis, benefactors? And what are the Russians and the Poles, philosemites? If we had no enemies, why did our ancestors leave the Promised Land?" I had never heard Finkelstein in such a rancorous mood. He must have had a fight with Heda.

"There is no promised land, only a fulfilled land, Mr. Finkelstein. The reference to a promised land was a place where aspirations of Jewish peoples for freedom from Egyptian bondage could be fulfilled."

"That's a fresh interpretation, Lev. Where did you read it?" asked Mi Kravitz.

"It just came to me. I make no claim to scholarship, Mi."

"This is all interesting," said Nudelman, "but we have business to conduct."

Schweig jumped out of his seat like a roman candle. "This is the business, Mr. Nudelman. The director has taken on himself the task of bringing peace to the troubled Holy Land by way of this obscure corner of Pennsylvania," he said, his voice shaking.

"There's nothing obscure about Western Pennsylvania, Mr. Schweig," pronounced Finkelstein, taking on even his ally in defense of the motherland.

"Don't let Mr. Schweig mislead you." Harney waded in. "His opinion doesn't represent the whole faculty."

"Harney is an apologist for the PLO," shouted Schweig. "If he hadn't run out on Israel, he'd be in prison."

Harney turned beet red, flew out of his seat and drove his fist into Schweig's eye and nose with a crackle. Schweig flew back, staggered, tripped and hit the floor with a thud. It was so unexpected that at first everyone was frozen, then several of us jumped up and converged on Schweig, relieved to see him stir.

Lev took charge and bending over, he called Mr. Schweig as if he were summoning him from the other side. Harriet Rosenzweig produced a chair cushion and slid it under Schweig's head.

"His nose is bleeding," said Nudelman. "Get some towels,"

"And some ice," said Lev. Mi Kravitz rushed toward the door colliding with a chair.

I looked up at Harney standing over our huddle. His jaw was rigid; his fists were still clenched. No doubt he was hoping Schweig would get up for a second round.

Nudelman took out his handkerchief and began to sop up the blood, which was tricking across Schweig's cheek. Mi returned with the ice and Gene Karp, who agreed to drive Schweig to the hospital emergency room. Schweig staggered to his feet, holding the towel and a plastic bag of ice, and left the room without a word.

Everyone looked at each other.

"Do we dare continue?" said Nudelman as he walked back to his seat. "Lev, you can see that your Palestinian recognition program isn't exactly going down like chicken soup."

"All the more reason to do it." Lev looked distressed by what had happened, a little grey, but he was composed, and his voice was level. He looked at Harney with sad compassion and said, "I know your feelings, but that was not the right reaction."

"I'm sorry. But what he said was so offensive."

"You should simply have let him go on. He would not have helped his point of view. By acting as you did, you hurt your own position."

"I should have turned the other cheek?" Harney had calmed down. No longer offended and exhaling smoke, he seemed now to be seriously evaluating his action as if none of us were present, except for Lev, who held Harney with his honest gaze.

"Better than to bruise his."

"Well," said Nudelman loud enough to break in, "let's get on with the business, now that Mr. Schweig's opinion has been handled." In truth, Nudelman didn't much care for Schweig. Isaac thought he was a twit.

For my part, what had happened was typical of any subject that was more emotion than reason. I was convinced that Palestine Day, or whatever it was, would only be bad if people made an issue of it.

"Go on with this program," said Finkelstein, his tone almost confidential, "and you will lose the school more than you hope to gain, Lev."

"We must take the risk, Mr. Finkelstein. All new ideas have difficult births. Did you know that drinking coffee was against the law when it was first introduced?" So Lev knew about that too!

"Next you'll be advocating the legalization of drugs," said Rabbi Bing, who had strong opinions on the subject since his oldest son had been arrested for possession his junior year at Columbia.

"Wrong thinking is the worst kind of drug, Rabbi," Lev responded.

"Having beaten that item to death, I suppose we should move on to something controversial," said Nudelman with a pained smile.

Harriet Rosenzweig looked up. "Not before we decide whether to override Lev's decision."

"Lev is the director. This is intended to be educational. We hired him to run the school. I say we don't interfere."

"Thank you for your confidence, Mr. Nudelman."

This time no one disagreed.

Before we could get onto another topic, Rosenzweig appeared in the door, collar open, blue and white tie askew, shirt damp with sweat, as though he'd run all the way from the courthouse. His leather briefcase was bulging and dangled from his right hand, making his shoulder droop with the weight of it. The lion has eaten Androcles, I thought.

"Well," said Nudelman looking apprehensive. "What happened?"

"Nothing's final. It's only a temporary injunction. But I'm afraid we didn't prevail entirely, not as to the critical elements of the case at least, although nothing is final and conclusive and there are other options but—" He let his briefcase drop with a thud and fell into a chair. His fleshy face was suddenly burning with irritation. "The judge hadn't read my brief; that was obvious. And he was so obsequious to that Herb Kleman, you would of thought they were lifelong pals."

"So what did he do exactly, in a few understandable words?"

"He tied up the endowment. We can go on with the school, but we can't use the interest on the $2 million. At least not until the trial is concluded, or we settle. Maybe they'll settle." His voice deflated like an untied party balloon. "Sorry. I did what I could." He raised a hand with a limp gesture of surrender.

I had never seen Rosenzweig so humble. At least some good had come out of it. Faced with this disaster, the matter of Palestine Day had shrunk to the importance of a flat tire when you're not in a hurry. As for the others, Nudelman, a businessman used to adversity, was working with a pencil on the notepad in front of him, already calculating a new budget no doubt.

Rabbi Bing seemed to be enjoying a moment of secret pleasure. Lev looked as though he hadn't even heard it, for he was chatting with Roe about the need for a computer.

Nudelman thought it best to adjourn the meeting and develop a plan. After a shock like this, a committee is worth even less than when it comes at a problem armed with information and forethought. I must confess that the disclosure didn't take me by surprise. But then I'm from the old world where disasters happen to people all the time.

People left the room chatting with that reserved don't-disturb-the-gods attitude that sometimes accompanies tragedy. I walked up to Lev, who was shuffling a few papers into an open file.

"What do you think?"

"Roe says he can get us a used computer from the insurance company. It will make some of the boys happy. They like it more than baseball."

"No, I mean the court case."

His answer was to raise both of his eyebrows, making five waves in his forehead. He let his breath out and touched my hand.

"Now we'll really find out how much the community wants to have a Jewish school."

## FIFTEEN

# Light in The Darkness

L ev's last words, as the tumultuous Board meeting ended,
echoed in my head like the aftermath of a shotgun blast.
What would the community do when the school was no longer a matter of moving existing money from one purse to the
other? With the practical efficiency that marked everything he
did Nudelman got out a letter to the synagogue membership,
followed by a telephone chain seeking contributions. Naturally
I was drafted to make some of the calls. After all the years as
the major domo of the synagogue I could just about do this in
my sleep.

Let me confess to you that I have never liked calling
someone and pulling them away from their favorite raisin
and noodle pudding or ritual weekly TV show to ask them
to increase, by five percent, their contribution to the Welfare Federation, the Building Fund, the Hospital Fund, the
Refugee Resettlement Fund, the National Fund, and so on.
I began to imagine that people, seeing me on the street or at
an *Oneg Shabbat*, holding a little plastic cup of sweet wine,

would tremble with apprehension or turn away, even if I said something like, "So how's Billy doing at college?" It came to me that inside his head was, "What next? Is Chaim about to ask for a contribution to the School, which once more was unable to pay the electric bill?"

But somebody has to do it. After all, I've never asked for a nickel for myself, which explains why I would be hard pressed to pay for a vacation in nearby Slippery Rock.

Anyway, catharsis behind me, the usual crowd and I made our calls, and what an earful we got from some. When you ask for money, people's complaints come out. Not that they are looking for an excuse not to give, it's just that they want you to know that it's even more generous of them to give their twenty-five dollars when they don't agree with anything that's going on but even so—. Well, I don't have to go on, for some of you have heard it and others have said it even while you are licking the envelope.

Aside from all the complaints, mostly about the Palestinian thing, people were generous, and some money was raised, although not enough. It's never enough, but people did respond to the crisis. People like emergencies. It makes them feel good that it's happening to someone else, but I am unkind.

Of course, the school was taking its own steps to deal with the new austerity. About twenty-five percent of the salaries were deferred, which didn't help morale on the faculty. Even teachers had rent to pay and other expenses, already hard to meet on half of what a bus driver makes.

Why is it that people must accept low wages to do things they love? If that's the rule, then why don't the real estate developers and bank presidents take deep cuts in salary if they like what they are doing, and if they all say that they don't like what they are doing then why don't they stop?

Besides raising money, I went out to the school once or twice. The mood was tubercular, which is to say it ranged from gloomy and angry to flushed and euphoric. You would think it was London during the Blitz. Why there were even plans being hatched in the computer room—Roe had come through with one—where all I could see were knowing smiles and whispers. Kids always have their secrets. And as for Lev, he was the calm in the eye of the tornado and went on personally planning what had been diluted to Nationality Day.

With a mixture of curiosity and anxiety, I went to the school for the program. Anyone with children knows the kind of event that I expected to see, with every student of every class doing a little something, even if it were no more than twirling in a circle and sitting down. Whatever they do, parents like to see their kids on a stage.

My first shock, in a way a thrill, was to see the blue and white Israeli flag draped outside the gothic doorway of the building alongside an unfamiliar red, black and green flag. Although I had never seen it before, I knew what it was—the intended flag of Palestine. Here was a bold dream, a vision of the future, a hope that carried, for me at least, nothing short of the lion and lamb image.

As far as I knew it was a first, this mutual flag hanging, for in Israel even to fly the Palestinian flag was to invite an indefinite vacation at a detention camp at government expense. Our little school had made symbolic history. If nothing else it might be remembered for this gesture, I thought. Little did I know.

Inside the building naive paintings of the nationalities aspiring to self- rule lined the hallways, with the most space devoted to the long history of the Jewish return to the Promised Land; photos of early settlers clearing swamps, walking on sandy streets of early Tel Aviv, all very evocative. Then there were pictures of Palestinians streaming out of villages, of black South African townships, of Armenians, Kurds, Lithuanians, and others. Children walked about in ethnic costumes made in art class.

I went into the great dining hall now arranged as an auditorium with rows of folding chairs and the massive tables moved against the walls. Nasal music, Middle Eastern, was coming from the speakers. A few parents were already waiting. Among them was Mumzer Arakat. He saw me, waved and pointed to an empty seat. I joined him, aware that some people would take it to be a political gesture on my part.

One look at Mumzer convinced me that, whatever came of it, Lev had been right. Mumzer made me a present of his tearful joy as he wrapped me in a brotherly embrace and planted a kiss on my left cheek. It was as if, for him, for the moment at least, all the hatred and mistrust between his people and mine was melting like spring snow. His friendship and gratitude passed through me and left me moist eyed.

"I could never imagine what is happening here today, Chaim."

"Yes, me too."

We gazed at each other, sharing our unspoken mutual dream of peace as the room filled with parents, and to my surprise, a lot of town people, people I knew to be active in their churches and helping organizations for the most part. I waved to Reverend Clarence Cantwell, pastor of the Bethel AME. He had played with Nudelman on the Bolton High basketball team and later marched with King in Alabama. Over the years I saw the same faces, a little older but marked by the same goodwill creases. I saw them at the meetings scheduled to do something about the schools, the air pollution, or starvation wherever it is happening. The people who attend are every color and religion, but they share a common humanity and compassion.

A few members of the Board came in together, a little late, looking apprehensive but clearly interested. I waved to Finkelstein and I could see that he hadn't decided whether to be scared or proud.

Mumzer and I fell into small talk; health, business, and pretty soon, the room hushed and the program began with a scratchy tape of the always-moving *Ha Tikvah*, the Israeli national anthem. While this was playing, two children marched down the aisle carrying between them a large poster painted with the seal of the State of Israel, the seven-branched *menorah*. Without a pause another tape, this one Middle Eastern. Mumzer leaned over and whispered, "It's the Palestinian national song." Two boys—his son, Sami, and Isaac Nudelman—came down the aisle. They were wearing identical checkered *kaffiyeh* and carrying a poster with a live oak and the Palestinian colors. This brought on a murmur from the audience, and in me, another wave of sentiment at the sight of these two friends and of the promise of trust.

It went on like that with African songs, an Arab dance, and a recitation of some poetry in Yiddish, Hebrew, and English, all about a yearning for a homeland. Who could miss the point? Only the blind and deaf.

Just when we thought the program was over, Lev went to the podium, limping slightly. He gazed about the audience with a look that was both abstract and intense. His eyes seemed lit by a distant fire. He had some notes with him, three pages, folded irregularly, and he glanced at them before speaking. He began slowly, with hesitation, as if he were searching somewhere inside him for the thoughts. Once begun, he seemed so fluent that he might have been speaking in his own language, except for the grammar and pronunciation. Not that what he said was emotional. Rather it was dry but there was something to think about.

Love was what he talked about first. Not sensual love, rather the attributes of the love of a mother for a child: forgiveness, sacrifice, tolerance. Against this he contrasted the rivalry of brother and brother, Cain and Abel, Jacob and Esau, the rivalry of princes for the crown, of politicians for office, of nations and those, who would be nations, for land. He stopped, looked through his notes as if he had lost his line of thinking. The audience waited. "Friendship," he said, and he likened it to mother love, derived, as it is, from an extension of self.

Nations, religions, language, culture, all divide people by keeping them from understanding their common humanity. Yet every person wants the same thing: love and security for themselves and a better life for their children. "What we must give to the stranger is not just hospitality or courtesy or even charity. We must give the stranger the same quality of understanding and active care we give to our own children." With that thought he stopped talking and his eyes seemed to fill with light, or so it seemed to me. Then he sat down and wiped the sweat off of his forehead with an unused ironed handkerchief.

Someone coughed. There was a crackle of applause, hesitant at first then gathering as others affirmed the good of what he had said. He smiled—a laughing, self-congratulatory, very human smile—and it was over.

As we stood amid the rattling of folding chairs and scuffling of feet, Mumzer turned to me and said, "He has a good head on his shoulders, don't you think, Mendel? But maybe he should have just left it to the kids."

"I don't know," I said.

I cut through the parents congratulating their children, and wished that one of them were mine. Weaving through the chatting clusters of parents and teachers I caught up with Nudelman, eager to hear his reaction to the speech, and even more, to the side by side flags, not to mention his son carrying the Palestinian emblem. He was just going through the door, shoulder to shoulder with Finkelstein. Isaac was already rushing down the hall with a gang of his friends.

"What do you think, Nudelman?" I asked, touching him on the shoulder of his beige tweed jacket.

"Interesting," Nudelman replied. "There were some warm touches among the children, don't you think?" He was subdued.

As for Finkelstein, all he would say was, "The flag was a lousy idea."

"What did you think about Lev's remarks?" I asked.

"Remarks?" said Finkelstein, pushing back his wiry red hair and looking like he'd just sucked a lemon, "You'd think he was the first person in the world to discover love. He should have been a rabbi."

"He held the audience too long, on those folding chairs." said Nudelman. "He seems to consider himself a prophet."

"I think he's just trying to get us to apply the fundamentals of Judaism on a broader scale," I said.

"Love your neighbor as you love yourself. The trouble is not enough people like themselves," said Finkelstein, his tone unusually snappy. And with that we separated.

I said hello to a few more people but decided to end my survey. All the same I was eager to kick the whole thing around with Estelle, but I held off leaving, for I also wanted to speak with Lev. I looked around for him, but he had disappeared. Selma Novik told me that he had gone to his rooms with one of those headaches.

# SIXTEEN

# Portents

Nationality Day might have passed, leaving a residue of goodwill, and some of the Board would no doubt have even considered it good for the school and the community, if a reporter for the *Bolton Daily Eagle* hadn't taken a picture of the two flags. Nothing much came of it, at first. The social page reported a good attendance at Nationality Day, an event held by the new Jewish school. The picture would simply have gone into the school's file if a cub reporter hadn't seen it upside down on the editor's desk and understood the significance of it.

"File this," said Sam Guthrie, the Editor-in-Chief, around the stub of his cigar.

The news reporter Morley Rasmussen just looked at him.

It should be said about Guthrie that international news in the Daily Eagle was confined to earthquakes, hurricanes, and the occasional birth of a two-headed lamb in Armenia. But Rasmussen had just gotten out of Penn State with a degree in Political Science.

"Excuse me, Sam," (everyone called him Sam)." Do you happen to know what we've got here?"

"Just a couple o' flags."

"This is the Palestinian flag, and this is the Israeli flag," said Morley, stabbing his finger at the photo.

"So?"

"This is probably the first time in history that the two have flown together."

"So?"

"It's wire service stuff, Sam, international news. Do I have to get you a background paper from the State Department?"

A bell rang in Sam's head. He remembered the last time Bolton had been on the international wires, the time some rabbi claimed he could cure people of cancer.

"They've gone and done it again," he muttered, a smile twisting around his cigar.

"Done what?"

"Nothin'. You think you got a story. It's yours. Write it and put it on the wire."

"With my byline?"

"You bet. It's your story."

And his story it became. Morley Rasmussen was no fool and he decided to make the most of his opportunity. So, instead of popping the cork and letting the fizz out right away, he went to the library and did a little research on the PLO and Israel. Just enough to put some flesh on the bones of his story, so that, should the big newspapers pick it up, they wouldn't dismiss it as the work of some small-town garden party writer.

He found out, to his growing satisfaction, that it was actually a crime for Palestinians to display their flag and that

Israelis could go to jail if they even said shalom to an official of the PLO. He called Lev and talked with him on the phone, looking for a nice quote. Then he tapped out the story in the empty newsroom on his IBM clone, stopping only to drink the remains of the day's coffee, as thick as gravy, and chat with Lord Nocklby, the cleanup man, who had once played third base for a Pirates farm club in Florida.

Morley told me that he had spent three times normal with the story, before he capped it with the simple headline "Jewish School Flies PLO Flag" and put it on the wires, feeling the mixture of relief, satisfaction, and fatigue that follows a sustained effort. He was a Lutheran and not given to excesses of faith, but he confessed to me that he said a little prayer to his blue-eyed God that the world would open its big eye to the story, that it would add a little to trust, and even make Morley Rasmussen famous for a day or so.

It was now day three after Nationality Day and Nudelman was breathing easier. He had gotten a call from Father Shanahan praising Lev and the Board for their courage and open-mindedness. Father Shanahan's brother was Nudelman's service manager. That made Nudelman feel good, until he got another call from Harry Blatt who thought that Lev Kyol should be fired for the outrage to the State of Israel. Harry's uncle taught Talmud in an orthodox yeshiva in New York and he didn't have much sympathy for the Palestinian cause. There were others like Harry's call, but fewer than he had expected. As yet he hadn't heard from the establishment in Pittsburgh although he was expecting a reaction. Other than the parents, only a few members of the Jewish community had attended, the ones who, more or less, believed in what the event stood for.

Of course, nobody on the Board knew that Morley had lit the fuse of a bomb. And explode it did, the next day on the front page of the *Pittsburgh Post Gazette*, and even on page 12-A of the *New York Times*, and so on, complete with the picture, and with Morley's byline no less.

Strange what a little official attention does. People don't form events, the media does. More precisely, life through the cyclopean eye of the media is more a collage of pieces or a crazy quilt, the kind made from leftover rags. So, it was with the Nationality Day.

Lev's telephone began to ring non-stop with people praising him or denouncing him. A television crew drove all the way from Pittsburgh and poked about the school doing 30 second interviews with a few of the teachers, old folks, and kids. They even talked to Lev, who spoke simply of the need for understanding and trust in the world, and especially in the place that gave birth to the first city and nurtured three of the world's religions. That quote played on TV on the six o'clock news and even more people found out what had happened.

The next day the local TV feature was distilled to a 30-second spot on the six o'clock national news, with a 10-second sound bite of Lev, a picture of the two flags side by side, and five seconds of thanks from the PLO observer to the UN.

With that, the media went on to other excitement—some sad nut had shot up a post office. Morley went back to something more interesting and exciting to the people of Bolton, the high school football team's shot at the state championship. The attention given the two flags lasted about as long as the reflection of lightning in a window, nothing like the time Rabbi Newman had cured cancer.

Then the ripple effect began to grow. Nudelman got a letter from the Israeli ambassador expressing his concern that "actions such as this by a school officially sanctioned by the Jewish community could be taken as ex-officio recognition of Palestine as a state, undercutting the State of Israel's efforts to achieve a just peace."

Suddenly anybody who was at all interested in the Palestinians and the Israelis was looking, with either a jaundiced or an approving eye, at the courageous or malicious, political or rash, altruistic or symbolic act of flying those two flags side by side. As if the two peoples weren't flying side by side in the Holy Land. From an eccentric, obscure educator, Lev had suddenly become a diabolical, socialist dupe, a naive and irresponsible idealist, and a courageous advocate of brotherly love and understanding.

# SEVENTEEN

# Pseudepigrapha

"Winter—the pale-blue tread of a rubber boot on fresh snow. The town seemed to shrink into the fold of the valley, a study in white, grey, and black. The trees, black against the snow, managed to save a few twisted brown leaves to remind them of the summer and looked like they wished they could board a tourist flight to Florida or California. Fresh snow, blended with salt and ash into a grey sherbet, spewed across the legs of shivering pedestrians, leaving stains on women's stockings and long coats. The mill, grey-smeared, its windows black, hiding its fires, belched white vapor into the lumpy sky—smoke scrubbed clean but smelling like ammonia."

No, it's not me. It's the words of Roy Fischback, one of the kids. An essay he wrote for ninth-grade English. More about him later.

Roy was right about that winter. For six days in January the temperature got no higher than six degrees. The sky was an infinite blue, and Frank's Body Shop was overflowing with bent fenders and stove-in grills from the black ice on the hilly streets.

The Monoganessen River, running like ink in December, froze over in January, and kids played hockey under the Main Street Bridge. More snow fell that winter than I can remember. Frank Manczyski, who owned the Shell station, made a fortune shoveling drives with his three plows.

Lev was happy. He liked the snow and the cold. "Just like *Moskva*!" he exclaimed, scooping up a handful of snow.

A thaw came in February and rows of long icicles formed on the edges of the roofs like eel's teeth. Rain gutters crashed screaming into the snow, under the burden of ice. One of them sent Avram Gan to the hospital with a concussion.

At the school, Roy Fischback and Sami Arakat climbed onto the sloping slate roof and nearly fell three stories trying to dislodge several of the icicles. Having salvaged five of them, which plummeted point first into the snow, they returned to the ground by way of the attic, a hangout for the Macabee Club. Roy was the colonel. Back on the ground, the Macabees engaged the rival club, the Zealots, in flailing, medieval combat using the icicles as swords and lances, not to mention snowballs with stone cores. Only one boy was injured, requiring only three stitches in his scalp. Roy struck the blow.

Of all the troublemakers, and there were quite a few, Roy Fischback was the gold medalist. Tall for his age, broad-shouldered, a real Aryan-type, with blond straight hair that fell over his forehead, except that he was all Jewish. Roy was as restless as he was strong. It was hard for him to sit through class. My Uncle Mayer would have said the boy has ants in his pants. Roy was always picking a fight, mostly with the other troublemakers. He wasn't a bully. He just liked to challenge others, a little like a ram in mating season.

His father was a Marine colonel stationed at El Toro, wherever that is. Although he wouldn't say, the psychological record in his file alluded to the fact that his father had employed some punishments that would have been the subject of an inquiry if he had used them on recruits. But Roy wasn't a recruit in Colonel Fischback's outfit; he wasn't even a volunteer.

Roy had been sent to our school after having been put on probation at his local public school for repeatedly brawling and giving his homeroom teacher the lip. He had also been caught with some pills in his locker—don't ask me what they were. I can tell you what they were not; they were not aspirin. On top of it all he had taken the football coach's Harley-Davidson for a joy ride.

And yet to brand Roy as just a troublemaker tells only part of his story. That should be obvious from his little essay. People have many facets, often contradictory. He could be very charming, very funny, although sometimes his humor was out of place, and if he liked somebody, he was generous and protective of the friendship. He was that way with Robin Primak.

Robin was a very shy, homely boy with bad skin, not very good at athletics, an off-key singer, terrific at math. In short, a person who nobody would pick as a best buddy, let alone to be part of a gang. He came from a broken home. His mother was an advertising executive in Detroit; his father lived in New Haven. He seldom got mail.

"Robin has been filed here," Lev told me one day, "under *E* for education."

Robin had one friend, one protector: Roy Fischback. If a kid called Robin "moon face" or "schmuck" when he tried to kick a soccer ball and missed, kicking his teammate instead,

Roy always came to his defense. They had nothing in common. Roy was arrestingly handsome, Robin unappealing. Roy was athletic, Robin inept. And Robin didn't even share Roy's talent for writing. Even so you could see that there was a bond between them of the same sort I felt for Lev. In their case it was a bond woven out of common fabric: family rejection. They supported each other against a hostile world. Adversity can be the leaven of friendship; it was with them.

So it went until one of the boys' wristwatch disappeared from his room. A few days later, a gold pen, then a twenty-dollar bill from a boy's wallet. The thefts were announced at the morning flag raising and prayer. The guilty party was told to return the items anonymously by leaving them in Lev's mailbox. Nothing turned up. So Lev, Bron, and Shusterman held a confab. Bron, was in charge of discipline. They suspected Roy, of course. They called him in. He denied having any part of it.

A week passed. Everybody took to hiding their valuables, some bought padlocks. Then one of the boys, the one who had the stitches from the icicle, reported seeing Robin Primak leaving the room of the boy who had lost the watch on the day it was reported missing.

Bron and Maimonides searched Robin's room while he was in class and found the watch hidden under his mattress. They reported back to Lev.

"What do we do, expel him?" they asked.

"Just the opposite," said Lev. "We honor him."

Lev appointed Robin Primak the school ombudsman with the responsibility of mediating any student's complaint about an unfair grade. He also made him senior math tutor. About a week later the stolen items turned up in Lev's mailbox. There were no more thefts.

That's not the end. Roy had his own problems. He had been warned and counseled again and again by Mr. Bron to avoid fighting, even if provoked. Bron was a tough cookie with the scars to prove it. He liked Roy and Roy knew it. Besides, Lev insisted that all criticism be given with warmth and support.

"We must bring out the good," he always said.

The icicle battle had passed with little comment. After all, boys will be boys and the Macabees and Zealots didn't use switchblades or chains, just fists. But when Roy broke a student's nose, someone who had responded in kind to one of his taunts, Bron and Lev decided something more had to be done.

"Expel him? I've run out of words," asked Bron.

"No," said Lev.

"What else is there to do? I've run out of kindness."

"I have something else in mind. Leave it to me."

Bron told me that Lev would say no more.

The next morning at prayer and flag raising Lev came out carrying a heavy walking stick; the Irish would call it a *shilehagh*. Seeing it, Bron wondered if Lev had corporal punishment in mind.

Once singing concluded, Lev asked Roy to come forward. The boy hesitated. Lev asked again, and Roy walked to the center of the ring, his face hard and fearless, no doubt expecting to be lectured, humiliated, or even beaten.

Lev stared into his eyes for a long enough time to make Roy squirm. Still saying nothing, Lev handed him the walking stick.

Roy took it, his expression melting into confusion. Lev bent over and clasped his hands to his forelegs.

"Beat me," he said. Roy stood there dumbstruck. A vacuum of suspended silence enclosed the circle of students and teachers.

"I order you to beat me with the stick," said Lev, his tone firm. Roy's arm went up halfway then fell back.

"Go on," Lev insisted.

Again, Roy's hand rose then stopped, as if some force kept it from going further.

"Well?"

"I can't," Roy said, his voice hardly audible and breaking with emotion. "I can't." He dropped the stick and ran through the circle.

Lev unbent his body, dropped his hands to his sides. His face was serious, calm, and intense.

"Time for class," he said, and the circle dissolved into twos and threes until only Lev and Mr. Bron were left standing next to the flagpole. Bron looked at Lev with skeptical awe.

"What made you do that?"

"What else could I do?"

Roy never struck another kid.

# EIGHTEEN
# Old Friends

It was Nudelman on the phone.

"Come to dinner tonight. Bring Estelle." This was no social call; it was the colonel summoning his junior officer. I pushed aside an article I was writing on early Jewish settlers in Western Pennsylvania. The affair of the two flags was still simmering. I was trying to stay out of the middle, like the jury that came back with the decision "not to mix in"—one of Rosenzweig's jokes. Rumors were flying as the song title goes. Everyone had an opinion. Lev was off his trolley, self-destructive, you name it.

Estelle cancelled her bridge game to come. She and Sarah Nudelman were tennis partners and went to an aerobics class once a week. She would never admit it but rumor had it that she was giving Nudelman tips on the market. According to Finkelstein, who shared the same stockbroker with Estelle, she was averaging an astonishing twenty percent return on her portfolio, a small-town Bernard Baruch.

There we were, sitting around Nudelman's glass coffee table looking through it at the brushed aluminum legs and the

Indian rug in some nice pastel colors, drinking a California wine that Sarah said had just been served at the White House. Why she cared I don't know, the President after all wasn't of her political party. Being with these people was to me as easy as being alone. We went way back, the four of us, and the three of them, all Bolton-born, went back even further. We were like family—familiar, tolerant, indifferent—taking each other for granted, so comfortable around each other that we could sit and say nothing.

"You are the two most level-headed people in the community," said Nudelman, looking at Estelle and me as if he meant it.

"What about Sarah?" asked Estelle, watching her friend as she went into the kitchen. "I like your new dress. Where did you get it?"

"Kaufman's."

"OK, three. But you two happen to be the closest people to Lev Kyol."

"Not me. Estelle," I said.

Estelle raised her glass and did a little half-bow. She was looking good. She had lost some weight and her black silk dress was pinching the right places. Maybe it was her fragrance, the smell of a soda fountain cherry Coke, that was getting to me. I've always liked that smell, since the first time Nudelman bought me one at Mary's.

"What's with Lev?" Nudelman finally said, his mouth still full of a Ritz cracker and sardine paste.

I shrugged, and Estelle shut down all expression except for the worry in her eyes.

"So?" Nudelman said, looking expectant. No response. He picked up a folded letter, and smiling a little, read it to us. It was from the Greater Western Pennsylvania Jewish Federation to the Board advising them that "in light of its rash and destructive recognition of Palestinian national identity" the Federation would not consider any further assistance to the school.

"You seem amused, Nudelman." I said.

"It's kind of ironic. You see, we had asked for help and they had already turned us down."

"Now they have a reason," said Estelle. "Sarah," she shouted. "Come out of the kitchen. Have some more wine! Visit!"

"And who will cook?" came a vexed voice from the kitchen. "Isaac! Get your fingers out of that icing!"

Isaac exited from the kitchen wearing a green sweat suit and licking his fingers. He noticed us and mumbled a shy greeting to Estelle and me.

"There's more," said Nudelman, drawing his lips back and squinting. "As you might imagine, ever since Harney KO'd Schweig in the first round, Schweig has been on the war path."

"Heda Finkelstein told me," said Estelle.

"And what did she say?"

"He's trying to get Lev deported."

"Just what I heard."

"On what basis?" I asked. Estelle was looking like she wanted to say something.

"That's what I want you to find out, Mendel."

"Now look, Nudelman!"

"It's for everyone's benefit, Mendel." He knew I would help.

When I made no more protest, he nodded with satisfaction. Mandy the dog got up from where she had been dozing under the baby grand piano and put her head on Nudelman's knee. He offered her a cracker with sardine paste. She sniffed it and turned away looking bored.

"Mandy's holding out for roast beef," said Nudelman.

"You spoil that dog," said Estelle, possibly for the one-hundredth time.

"Mandy's old, Estelle," Nudelman answered ritually for the one-hundredth time. "Any idea what's up Schweig's sleeve, Estelle? Has he got something on Lev?"

"Why ask me?"

"You're Lev's confidant. You do his laundry."

"That's a *non sequitur*, if I ever heard one." Estelle had been on the high school debate team and she still threw around phrases like that. "You think I would betray him if I knew something? What kind of friend would I be?"

"Just thought I'd ask. Sarah. When do we eat? The guests are getting testy."

"Patience," was the response from the kitchen.

"There is some good news," said Nudelman, pouring each of us some more wine. "Izzy Bortz and Gene Karp are each contributing $1,000 a month the school while the finances are tight."

"I hope you haven't tried to cash the check," I said.

"Why? As a matter of fact, we have. Why do you ask?"

"Only because, compared to them, I look like one of the Rothschilds."

"At this point, I'm not going to ask questions. We need every dollar."

"Dinner! Bring your wine glasses."

I got up wondering where the money had come from. Now I had something else to ask questions about.

"What's for dinner?" I asked.

"Standing rib."

"Mandy's favorite," said Estelle and she gave Nudelman an affectionate poke in the rib.

## NINETEEN

# Going Fishing

With all the goings-on, winter slipped out the back door like an unpopular guest at a party. Exhausted, grimy, the town waited for a revival of life as the last patches of snow shrunk under the assault of icy March rains. Storm windows were cracked open, salt was washed off the sidewalks and encrusted cars, and the Monogonessen rose against its brown banks. Gardeners watched for the first haze on the branches of the apple trees and searched the soggy flowerbeds for tines of green as the crocuses and daffodils emerged.

Week by week spring ripened: forsythia bushes blazed yellow against the still-dead grass, warm moist air followed cool gentle rain, until one day was so fresh with color and growth that I put off my usual work. I had planned to go to the school. First I would to play a little hooky—a funny American slang word, hooky, meaning crooked or devious according to the Oxford English Dictionary.

I turned down a dirt track for a mile or so to reach a deeply shaded hollow with a fast moving stream gushing white over smooth rocks. It was a favorite spot, especially in the spring. I took off my shoes and socks, rolled up my pants and chilled my feet in the water of what some people call Bridal Creek. I put my hands behind my head and lay back in the young weeds, smelling fresh leaves, water, wet humus and rock. I lay there, feeling the damp soil through my shirt, looking up through the translucent leaves at the dappling sunlight, and thought of my childhood beside another stream, long ago in another world.

Prufrock came to mind. It must have been the act of rolling up my pant legs. T. S. Eliot in Bermuda shorts walked through a door nodding his head. It was Lev Kyol. I must have dozed off. I could just lie here and forget the school for a day at least, I thought. I didn't really want to go out there and snoop around for gossip. It was against my nature. Besides, I might have discovered something that would make things even worse than they were turning out to be. Still, I wondered what, if anything, Estelle was holding back and if it had to do with Schweig's deportation plan.

The rush and murmur of the water and the undulant Birdcall from the trees again sent me off on a doze. The rumble and rattle of a tractor crossing the wooden bridge woke me with a start and, for an instant, I had the feeling I was someone else; who, I don't know. But it was only me—a little older with yet another spring behind me and my own spring even further back in my memory.

On to the school to spy on poor Lev, and perhaps to help him, but first I would chat with Selma Novik. I found her sitting on a bench on the front lawn. She was knitting what looked like the red sleeve of a sweater. In her pale blue cotton dress, a wide-brimmed straw hat shading her pale face, she was the aged eye of a storm of children. Swirling about her were kids, big and little—chasing each other, playing catch, shagging fly balls, kicking a soccer ball, slapping a volleyball back and forth over a net—all screaming and shouting.

"Mendel, how nice of you to come on such a grand April day. The sun feels so good on these old bones. After winter, it takes a month just to warm them up."

I sat down beside her, and she filled me in on the happenings. Miss Leventhal had fallen and broken her hip. The accident had made her even more forgetful, but what could you expect of someone in her late nineties. Selma was looking forward to the homeless dinner, although she didn't approve of Lev's menu. In fact, she planned to bake some tea cakes and surprise people with them, whatever Lev thought.

I steered the conversation to the finances, hoping that she would mention something about Izzy and Gene and their new-found wealth but if she knew anything she wouldn't say.

As I was about to get up I saw Gene Karp coming toward me, dressed, of all things, in one of those cotton baggy exercise outfits and bright blue rubber-soled shoes with red racing stripes. He was slim and might even have been a runner in his youth. His face was red and he was sweating. As always, I wondered whether he secretly died his thick black eyebrows and, if so, why didn't he also color what was left of his hair?

"Will you look at him," said Selma under her breath. "He thinks he's Jessie Owens."

"Training for the Olympics, Gene?"

"Mr. Bron, the athletic coach, has got us all doing some exercise, would you believe it. I am trotting around like an old dog. I even bought those fancy shoes I saw on TV, the ones that blow up inside. It's like walking on a cloud."

"If you're not careful, you'll blow up inside yourself," said Selma.

"Exercise isn't all that's new in your life, I hear."

The old suspicion returned to his face and he said, "What do you mean?"

"I hear you're making contributions to the school."

"That was supposed to be anonymous. We don't want any credit. There never were any secrets in this town. I remember the time some kid stole my car. Everybody knew about it before I did."

"I didn't know you were that well off," I said, feeling like a detective and not liking it.

"Nobody's business but mine."

"Izzy Bortz is giving money too, which is remarkable because he usually won the prize for giving the least of anybody."

"I guess he just likes it here and wants to help." Gene's mercury shoes looked like they wanted to take him someplace else.

" I think Izzy's getting some money from the insurance. Some policy that he forgot all about," said Selma.

"I'm going to be on my way," said Gene, and his magical shoes floated him back toward the building in a brisk, flat-footed walk.

There was something very peculiar about the fact that suddenly both Bortz and Karp had become such supporters of the school after all their complaints. A soccer ball rolled toward me. I stopped it with my toe and kicked it back. We used to play soccer in the D.P. camp but when I came to Bolton no one had even heard of it. Now it was becoming popular. Too late for me.

"Gene has always been close-mouthed," Selma recalled, going back to her knitting. "I remember when his wife died. You wouldn't remember her, Mendel. He wouldn't speak of it to anybody right away. I suppose he was afraid to let it out. Some people are like that."

I put the question of the sudden philanthropy out of my head for the moment and went inside to look for Schweig. I found him just as he was going into his office. He never looked happy, and now was no exception. It must be his narrow sloping shoulders and down turned eyebrows, I concluded.

His greeting, "Mr. Traig," was not exactly full of welcome. I asked to speak with him, and after sizing me up, he nodded and gestured me into his cluttered workspace. In the days of the hospital it had probably served as a spacious walk-in linen closet and nurse station.

"Sit down. What can I do for you?"

I had never much cared for him and didn't want to fuzz things up with small talk, so I just said, "Nudelman wants me to ask you if it's true you're trying to get Lev Kyol deported."

"Why doesn't he ask me himself?" Before I could answer he said, "He'll find out soon enough."

"I take it that's a yes."

No response, just a level look and a snort from his long nose.

"Why? Why are you doing this?"

"Look, Mr. Traig. My sympathies are with any Jewish refugee from persecution. But having endured this man for the last six or seven months, I'm convinced that he has no place

in Jewish education, here or anywhere. Maybe they do it differently in Russia but he's no educator." His face lacked feeling
but there was acid on his tongue.

"The Board thinks he knows his stuff. I know you have
strong feelings about the Palestinian issue."

"I confess I do. Most people do. Any teacher who sacrifices
income because they believe in Jewish education would." He
looked as though he were struggling within himself. His right
eyelid began to twitch. "I know, you think me to be malicious,
I can tell. You think my ideas are extreme." His rigid expression
broke into a gesture of a smile. He looked at me searching for
a response.

I said nothing, but I began to feel sorry for him. I finally
said, "I'm sure you have good reasons for feeling as you do." It
was so close in the room I was having trouble breathing. "You
know you ought to ask for a better office."

"I usually leave the door open. But you didn't come here to
improve my office. We were talking about Lev Kyol. Plainly and
simply, having listened to him and observed him, I'm convinced
that he doesn't know anything about learning, about curriculum, about collegiality, about state certification requirements.
He's a fraud. You've been fooled, all of you, the whole Board."

"That's your opinion."

"Not my opinion. Here look at this." He handed me a
typewritten letter. It was supposed to be a translation of Lev's
employment certification from the Ministry of Education. It
said that he had been superintendent, in Public School 49 for
the last ten years. I looked up, confused.

"What does this prove? It says he was superintendent?"

"Not director. Superintendent. Do you know what the superintendent is? He's the janitor. He makes sure the place is clean!" Schweig's face flushed with vindictive triumph.

My heart dropped into my stomach. On top of everything else, this! I should have stayed at Bridal Creek.

"You're saying he lied about his job to get into the country?" My voice was suddenly hoarse.

"See for yourself. And lying about your job is ground for deportation."

I just looked at him and felt as though the elevator on which I was riding had just snapped its cable. Even so, on the way down I wanted to chuckle at the deception. There were times in my life when I had thought that the credentialed people weren't all that suited to their jobs. That explained, in part at least, why Lev's point of view was so fresh. He wasn't burdened by convention at all. He was inventing education all over again, just as the Baal Shem Tov, Buddha, Mohammed, and Jesus had to conjure up a fresh view of faith.

A part of me wanted to say hurrah! A good reason to keep him on, but Schweig was already as raw as a peeled carrot. If I was going to have any influence it would be by taking a neutral approach.

"Shouldn't the Board handle the deportation question? After all, Mr. Schweig, fraud or not, he's still a Refusenik, a victim of persecution, and as a Jew you wouldn't want to send him back to Russia, would you?"

"He can always go to Israel. If he's so set on working with the Palestinians, he should move to Israel, shouldn't he? He can see for himself. He's not going to solve the problem here in Bolton. Sami's name is Arakat, after all, not Arafat." His attempt at a joke!

"Yes. Maybe that's the answer. Let him migrate to Israel. And in the meantime the Board would remove him and replace him with someone with the proper credentials, from the staff," I said.

Somewhere back in Schweig's head, a 60-watt light bulb went on and he said, "That should certainly be the first step. Letting him continue another day is a mockery. If word gets out, the school will look ridiculous. A janitor for a director!"

"It's original, you'll have to admit that," I said, searching for his funny bone.

"If it were a Marx Brothers film, it might be amusing." I studied him for a sign that the plaster of his intention was beginning to crack.

"Yes, he'll be happy in Israel. He might even find another job like this one." I tried again.

"Yes, Mr. Traig. There is a certain humorous element." The solemn, formal smile reached his eyes.

"Then I can have your promise not to pursue this until the Board has a chance to act? After all, it is their responsibility."

I waited. He nodded his head with a grave look.

"They should have a chance to be more responsible than they have been when they hired him. And, for that matter, when they misappropriated the trust fund." With that he got up and dismissed me. What a headmaster he would make—something out of Dickens. And yet for all his formality, I still felt sorry for him. Who was hiding behind that starched front? Someone who was afraid of the dark.

I had bought some time. I shook hands with a crestfallen Schweig and left his office with his tentative, narrow eyed smile probing at my back. What a relief! Another one they had hired from a photograph. I had no idea I could be so manipulative. It wasn't in my character. Damn Nudelman. Wait till he finds out. He should be doing this. After forty years I was still picking up his towels.

My next stop was Lev's office. Luckily, I found him hunched over his desk, for it saved my scouring the school for him.

If I had any animosity over his deception it melted when he looked up. He was weary-looking and that made me feel sorry for him, but he was also glad to see me, and that drew me to him. I've always liked people who show feeling for others. More than a smile I mean, for a smile is an easy mask—a shopping mall give-away to gain a little good will at no expense. Real feeling comes at a higher price.

"Mendel, my dear. You are looking good, or is it *well*? Well, to me, is not being sick. This English…"

If you don't watch out English will not be a problem, I thought.

"Tea? I make some," and he got up and began to fuss with the hotplate.

"Lev, I have a serious question." I decided to get right to the tip. I swallowed before asking, "What is a superintendent exactly in a Russian school?"

"I don't know, exact. Boss, maybe," he answered with his back turned—he was still mishing with the tea.

"It's not the person in charge of keeping the place clean?"

"More than that."

"It's not the same as the school director or head master or principal, is it?"

"Depends on school." He turned toward me, his face dead serious now, his eyes searching.

"Let me put the cards on the table. Schweig thinks you were the head cleanup man, not the director, back in Moscow. He thinks you lied to the Board."

Lev forgot about the tea, although the steam was already vaporizing, and the hot plate was bright orange.

"Truth is never so simple, Mendel."

"This is no time for philosophy, Lev. Schweig wants to get you sent back to Russia. Or maybe Israel."

"You think I lie, Mendel?" The question was quiet, composed.

"No. But you need to turn off the hot plate."

He looked surprised before he realized what I was saying. He calmly went back to making the tea while I waited for an explanation.

"I show you something," and he reached into his drawer and pulled out an envelope, yellow with age. From it he pulled an equally yellow document with an official seal. Though it was written in Cyrillic script I could see it was some sort of credential. "My degree from pedagogic institute. You see my name. I am qualified teacher."

"Good! I'm relieved. Then you were the director after all and superintendent was just a bad translation?"

"No. I was head of maintenance, as you say. Also holding books, supplies and such." He handed me a teacup with a solemn look, one that was devoid of shame or guilt.

"Why, if you were qualified to teach, did you choose to do this?"

"No choice in Soviet Union. I was Jew and also, I study and teach Hebrew. No job for me, except clean up."

"All the same, you claimed to be something else."

"No. I just say superintendent. I do not, did not lie."

There was nothing more to say. I was glad he had the right papers at least, but I knew the Board would have no choice but to give him the boot. And now it was my problem. How to save him? I wanted to. He deserved a chance to prove himself, a chance he'd never gotten before.

# TWENTY

# Not Even A Pillow

I rushed home from the school to the security of my book-lined apartment and defrosted a bagel. Somehow, when I am afraid, a hot bagel spread with cream cheese makes me feel a little better. The Scottish have their Scotch, the Irish their whiskey, the Germans their beer, and so on. For me the yeasty smell of a bagel and the bland taste, the deception of the brittle crust yielding to the soft flesh, bring me back to a time when my only troubles in life were getting my addition right so that Mr. Krupowski, my teacher, wouldn't rap me on the knuckles with his ruler. I suppose there's something metaphysical about a bagel: a dense substance, a circle and therefore eternal, like life's wheel, circling a void. But is it a void, the hole in the bagel, or is it rather the negative force that creates the bagel? Without the hole there would be no bagel. Once again, I go on about something else instead of the telephone call that I made to Nudelman.

Nudelman heard my report without getting excited—he was a cool one.

"At least he has a teacher's license," he said. "But we look kind of silly, not finding out what a superintendent is."

"Tell me, Nudelman, what will be your personal position? Will you recommend that they give him the boot?"

There was only silence, except for the hissing of the telephone line.

"Too soon to say. I've got to do what's best for the school, whatever I feel personally about him. What do you think we should do?"

"Keep him. He's special."

"Easy for you to say, Mendel. But I appreciate your input. And thanks for your help. In any event, I'm going to keep this under the hood until that dinner is over. Who knows, he might make some friends."

Next, I called Estelle, eager to get her reaction. She sounded like it was nothing new to her, which again made me wonder just how close she was to Lev. That must have been the secret she was holding back, I concluded.

Enough of that. It was time for me to order the monthly supplies for the community center. Our usual supplier had gone into bankruptcy. I had to find another one. Even when most of the people are doing fine, which means they are paying the bills and putting some away that doesn't go to taxes, others are going down the drain. Over in India a child is bitten by a snake, or shot by Muslim or Hindu extremists, while she is taking a train to visit grandma. In the Soviet Union, grandma is tearing up Pravda for toilet paper and slicing a fatty sausage for dinner. In Ethiopia, a family is huddling under a blanket; their only shelter and going without dinner altogether. All of those images running through my mind put my attempt to save three cents per roll on toilet paper into perspective. Even so, I found a new supplier in New Castle and saved three -and-a-half cents per roll.

For the next week I lay low, hoping nobody would get me deeper into the school mire. I drove into Pittsburgh to do some research at the University library and abandoned my intriguing theory that Daniel Boone was Jewish, having seen a copy of the entry of his birth in the family bible, the New Testament. Still it had been fun to theorize, and it wasn't the main thesis of my research. I was more interested in the letters and accounts of Mordecai Ruben, a fur trader. But the usual savor of a dim and dusty desk in a quiet library with a stack of crackling books to pore over was missing. Again I found myself worrying about Lev Kyol. Back at home I would wait for the telephone to ring with some news. I would repress my curiosity and go on about my business only to have the same anxieties return.

Went about my business, that is, until the night of the homeless dinner. I had expected to drive Estelle, but she begged off, saying she was busy. In truth I almost decided to be busy myself. A friend from Pittsburgh had offered me a ticket to *The Merchant of Venice*, but a call from Nudelman pinned me down. He was coming late, after some negotiations, and would I be there early to observe.

Despite my best intentions my car wouldn't start—a dead battery—and by the time I got there the great dining hall was nearly full. This time there were more people from the congregation. Whatever people thought about the stateless, they couldn't turn their backs on the homeless. And there were many more from other congregations: Mr. Kim, the Korean who was managing Nudelman's old store, a few Kiwanians and

Masons, and even the treasurer of the Steelworkers' Union, Kaszymr Polsky.

But what stood out most about the crowd was what usually might be called the people at the head table. There was room for nearly twenty, although I counted no more than twelve. This wasn't just a dinner to benefit the homeless. The homeless were the guests. A few of them I recognized. They could always be seen begging in the same places. One man, wrinkled as a walnut with a caved-in mouth, was always in the doorway of the old Kresge's, sitting on a square of corrugated paper, his back against the boarded-up window. There was a woman in her thirties with two blond children, shabby but scrubbed; a man with a raw wound over his distended right eye; a woman who had feathers in her tangled grey hair, and others—young, old, vacant in the eye, or excited and self-conscious, shaking or stiff.

It was shocking, even to me. They didn't belong here, I said to myself, but of course my reaction was wrong. They were among us and we couldn't deny their existence or raise money for them as if they lived in some African country six thousand miles away. These were our own people, yet for many reasons, none of them good, we had turned away from them.

I found a seat next to someone I was too fixated to even notice, as Lev walked to the podium.

"My friends," he said, "we are here today to help and honor our poor. I will not speak of them. It is they, your neighbors, who will speak, and you will hear from their own voices and souls who they are. But first we will take a meal together, all of us common brothers and sisters, bound together by our common humanity."

With that, he turned away, picked up a bottle of wine and began to pour a little for each of the people at the head table. Then he said the blessing over the wine and they drank. He chanted the blessing over the bread—a large braided challah—tore it into twelve pieces and gave one to each diner.

As if responding to a signal, the children appeared carrying pots and platters. Some went to the front, others passed among us giving us the meal Lev had promised: a thin barley soup with just a gobbet of chicken fat. That and a clod of course black bread, not even fresh.

The poor ate another meal that night; the one Estelle had cooked, Estelle and Sarah Nudelman. We could smell it as we ladled out thin tasteless soup and gnawed on the hard bread, so hard it hurt the gums to chew. The poor ate fatty roast duck with rich gravy and a savory stuffing, and there was a fresh vegetable salad and apple pie. They ate with exuberance. Even those who seemed not to be aware of where they were, were reanimated, as if something of their old life had returned to them. In fact, as the meal went on, the poor at the head table started to look like they belonged.

I looked around at the rest of us expecting to hear a few cynical comments or see angry, complaining looks. After all, the soup had cost thirty-five dollars. For the most part, there was goodwill and community among acquaintances and strangers.

The meal completed, the children passed among us clearing the tables, and without an introduction, the Kresge man stood up. He shambled to the microphone and began to speak in a rusty voice, one that might not have been used for a long time. He began with his name. He spoke simply. His father had abused him, he had been truant, stolen, been in jail, not held a job for more than a month. He wanted something better for himself but was glad just to stay out of the rain and fill his stomach. As a child he had dreamed of being a fireman, but he couldn't remember when he had stopped dreaming.

Next was the woman with the children at her side, one about six years old, the other about four. They clung to her hands and looked about them with solemn, sad faces as she spoke of a husband who had lost his job and left them, of eviction and of shelters, which were worse than the street. She had come to Bolton from Pittsburgh, hoping to find work as a waitress so that the children, at least the oldest, could go back to school. He was a good student, she said, a bright boy.

And so it went, one after the other they spoke before hushed witnesses. We left the room long after midnight and, for the moment, were changed. For a time we had become children again, at least in our capacity to feel. I didn't speak with anyone on the way out that night. I didn't want to dilute my feelings with words.

# TWENTY-ONE

# Looking For Signs

Charity, or rather help, works best when it's focused—
the child who needs the operation to save her life raises
more from sympathetic strangers than 200,000 anonymous
homeless children. So it was no surprise that word of mouth
combined with a local news item by Morley Rasmussen produced all kinds of assistance for the twelve homeless who had
told their stories. Offers of clothes, temporary jobs, places to
stay—humble but better than the street—all came in to the
school telephone operators. The old folks were taking turns
at this job.

The blond woman with the two kids, Donna O'Day, got
a job at the Koffee Kup as a waitress and an apartment above
someone's garage, with no deposit. Her children were both
enrolled, one in the elementary school, the other in a Baptist
pre-school. Even the Kresge's man, Elmo Riegle, was offered a
job washing dishes and a bed in the basement of the Holiday
Inn. One of the town councilmen came up with a proposal to
turn the closed Kresge's store into a help center with sleeping

space for the homeless, but it was referred to a committee for review and was never seen again.

As for our school board and the Jewish community, the dinner left everyone catching their breath from having been hit in the solar plexus. What Lev had done was so unusual and so full of symbolic and real compassion. Even the grumblers had to admit that his was a higher level of conscience and that while other do-gooders talked about it, he did it. The Board was proud of the school and proud of themselves.

The appreciation of the event and its results didn't stop in Bolton. Morley's article about the dinner was picked up on the wires and connected to the earlier two flag event. Letters began to arrive from all over the country wanting to know the details so that other groups could put on similar dinners for the homeless. At the request of a subscriber, *Gourmet Magazine* even wrote Lev asking for the recipe for his Poor Person's Soup.

Selma Novik and the old folks had a fine time answering the letters—they were now handling all of the clerical tasks at the school as well as the telephone. One of the children, Suzy Roe, did a linoleum block print of the recipe, ornamented with beets and carrots at the corners, and they sent it to everyone who sent in a contribution, even those who hadn't asked for it.

About two weeks later a letter came from a lady in Texarkana, Texas, saying that the soup had about cured her chronic ulcer. A man from Missouri claimed that the soup had virtually eliminated his insomnia.

These testimonials were bland compared to what was going on in Bolton. Elmo Riegle had begun to dream again. Not about being a fireman—washing dishes was as close as he would ever come to that. His dream, more a vision, was that Jesus had come back to earth in the person of Lev Kyol. How did he know this? Lev's handshake and his compassion, his sharing of the bread and wine, his speaking Hebrew, the language of the Bible, all were signs. And most importantly, his touch had restored Elmo's self-esteem, giving him strength to pull his life together. Since the night of the dinner Elmo hadn't had a drop of hard liquor, just a little Gallo screw-top Chablis with a friend, but not enough even to get a buzz on let alone pass out. He was shaving and showering every day and even reading the Holy Scriptures. A great peace had taken over his body and spirit and healed it, he claimed.

Elmo was a loner and, at first, the only people he told were his fellow dishwashers at the Holiday Inn, but they didn't speak English. Obsessed with the need to get the word out, one Sunday he put on a fresh white shirt and walked to the First Pentecostal church. When the time came for the testimonials he just got up and spilled the beans. As some of you know, the synagogue and the church share a parking lot. I can often hear the singing from my apartment when they get going, but this reaction sounded like it would blow out the windows. I almost went over to see what was up.

Morley Rasmussen got wind of the testimonial. He stopped work on a story about the new maternity wing of the Bolton Memorial Hospital and rushed out to the Holiday Inn. By now Morley was fixated on Lev Kyol. He was the bird on the back of the cow. He had been at the dinner, seen Elmo and the rest of them.

A Lutheran and a skeptic, Morley had never actually been touched by the warm hand of God, not that he didn't like a good sunset. He assumed that Elmo's booze-softened mind was giving him hallucinations. That's what he thought until he saw Elmo in his white apron with a partially washed pot in his hand. Now Elmo wasn't exactly that frog that had returned to being a young prince, but even matter-of-fact minded Morley could see that something significant had changed. Elmo's eyes were clear, there was a flush in his cheeks beyond the red arteriole tracks, and his words were pretty lucid. For whatever reason, Elmo was renewed. Morley diligently took down everything and drove out to see Lev—by now they were chatty friends.

I happened to be in Lev's office when Morley arrived with a bemused, incredulous look on his round, open face. It must have been hard for him to talk about Elmo's revelation in the same tone that he used to discuss the introduction of a new hybrid rose at Bolton Hills Nursery, but he tried.

"So that's what was going on at the Pentecostal church last Sunday," I said, and I told him about the extra noisy prayer meeting.

Lev was sitting in his squeaky swivel chair, his elbow on the desk, and his chin cupped in his palm. If he registered any surprise at the news that he had been anointed God's messenger on earth I couldn't see it. Morley might have been telling him about his TV conking out in the middle of *Masterpiece Theater*. His response was that of a career diplomat at a press conference.

"Some people are animated by visions. Some visions make them feel better, some make them feel worse," he said with a gentle, all-knowing look.

"Do you share in his vision?" asked Morley.

"Yes, I share it."

"You do?" Morley looked surprised. For my part, nothing surprised me about Lev anymore. His middle name was surprise. Even so, I would have expected a denial. What was he saying, that it was true?

"If that is what I am to him then that is what I am," he explained. "I cannot deny him his personal truth when it makes a change for the good in him."

"Then you are presuming to be God."

"Not God. An arm of God, in a metaphorical sense, that is."

Now I began to understand, at least I thought so.

"May I quote you?" Morley stammered. He was a smart young man but, like many people, he hadn't spent much time meandering in the labyrinth of the spirit. Besides, he had his piece to write.

"I said nothing that was worth repeating."

"All the same, Lev. You have added something to the story." And with that, Morley excused himself—he had a deadline to meet. I later heard he got a speeding ticket on the way back to the newsroom. He was too preoccupied to notice the radar.

"You have a strange effect on people, Lev," I finally said. "You can be so ambiguous, even a little prophetic."

"Mendel, my friend, I only try to be teacher. Now what is it you were talking about?"

"I was saying that Nudelman and most of the Board accepts why you were a superintendent rather than a teacher, let alone a director."

"Good."

"They can't fault you for being a Refusenik or for teaching Hebrew in your apartment. They don't want to claim that you lied to get into the country. That's it, in an eggshell, as they say."

"Then they will do something about this?" and he handed me a formal notice from the Immigration and Naturalization Service to show cause why Lev Kyol should not be deported for entering the United States by making false statements on his application and so on.

"Schweig!" I muttered.

"I wasn't saying anything."

*Schweig* was the Yiddish word for "be quiet," but it was also the name of that contemptible, deceitful, well—

"I'll give this to Rosenzweig; he'll handle it. Don't worry about it."

"Mendel, I am beyond worry." He stood up and put his hands together palms up, brought them to his lips and gave me a long, solemn look. His long hollow-cheeked face seemed to have a grey pallor but maybe it was just the lack of light in the room.

"That's good," I said, wishing that I could have said the same. Here were two more problems heaped like dry wood on the fire of controversy that could burn Lev, if not the whole school. Would the Board tolerate a latter-day Jesus as its director? The thought made me chuckle even while I quaked.

I parted from Lev and went after Schweig's scalp. I wanted to tell him what I thought of him before my blood cooled. Fortunately, he wasn't in his cubbyhole and I wasn't about to stalk him.

I went to my car and drove to Rosenzweig's office without even trying to cadge a fresh tea cake in the school kitchen. I was going to drop off the papers but as I came through the door of the reception area I saw him coming out of his inner office on his way to the men's room. I hadn't seen him in a couple of weeks and I was surprised see how thin he had become.

"Liquid diet," he said as he pointed to the fresh holes in his belt and gestured me toward the door of his office. The floor was like a minefield, only instead of mines there were piles of paper. I picked my way to a chair and sat down only to face a pile of files on the desk. Of all the men I know, Rabbi Bing was the only one who consistently kept a neat office. What did that mean? But I had already had my fill of speculation on the nature of humanity for the day.

I coughed and winced at the stale cigar smoke that permeated everything, even the files. Rosenzweig returned, belatedly zipping his pants.

"Be glad you are metabolically thin, Mendel," he said, falling back in his high-backed black leather swivel chair. "I suppose Nudelman told you," he added. He looked grave, although it might have been due to his sagging jowls.

"How did Nudelman know?" I asked.

"I told him."

"Who told you? Not Lev?"

"He doesn't know yet."

"Of course he does."

"He couldn't. I just got a call from the FBI."

It struck me that we weren't talking about the same thing. Yet another trouble. "You go first," I said.

"Know what a hacker is?"

"Somebody with a chronic cough?"

"No. It's a computer thief."

"On top of everything, somebody stole the school computer?"

"The other way around, Mendel." Rosenzweig's face took on the dramatic wide-eyed tension of shocking revelation. He must be good with juries, I thought.

"Somebody busted into the computer system at the insurance company and has been writing benefit checks in large amounts to people who shouldn't be getting them."

A burglar alarm went off in my head. "Don't tell me."

"You got it. Two of our old folks." He drew up his lower lip with his teeth.

"But they wouldn't even know how to turn a computer on."

"There's a kid at the school," said Rosenzweig with a nod, "a computer whiz. Then of course there's Suzy Roe, who could have helped."

I remembered seeing Isaac Nudelman at the computer, but I wasn't about to implicate him.

" The FBI suspects this kid?"

"He's on their hacker list."

"They are great list makers."

"This is no time to be funny, Mendel." Rosenzweig sat back with a grunt, a memory of when he had more weight to shift.

"While you're fretting, add this to the pile," I said, handing him the notice from the Immigration Service.

As he read it, he reached into his desk drawer and pulled out the biggest Hershey bar I've ever seen.

# TWENTY-TWO

# Edible Flowers

So there we were again, sitting across Lev's cluttered glass topped desk, sipping amber tea in glasses, the way the Russians did it. Lev looked as worn as a discarded tire. His eyes looked hollow with dark shadows that reminded me of Lon Chaney Sr. in *Phantom of the Opera*. But there was something powerful burning in those eyes, a laser—from what I've read of them—zipping through the labyrinth of his nerves. Not that it was scary, not at all. Rather it had the feel of a star pulsing so far away that it didn't make me squint. Yet knowing how far that light had come, through space, across time, I had a sense of cosmic power so great that I was both humbled and calmed at the same time. Aside from that, he seemed to be wasting away. It must have been the stress of events, one after another, all bad.

"You look like you haven't had a good night's sleep in a week."

"I never need much sleep, my friend." Lev's voice was distant, as though it was coming from some cave deep inside him.

"How are things here, since you've been appointed the Messiah and all?"

That made him smile in a very Jewish way—one that showed true amusement and sadness too at human foolishness beginning with your own.

He reached his long hand across the glass top of the desk, grasped a pile of letters three inches high, and held them up loosely so that several drifted out.

"You know how much money comes from strangers since Morley sent out his story? Take a guess, Mendel. Guess and you win another tea cake."

He watched me, rubbing his tongue across his front teeth, as I struggled to come up with a figure. I've never been good at such things, estimating the number of beans in a jar and such.

"Uh, $500 more or less?"

"About $25,000 from all over the country."

"Who from?"

"All kinds. Some give for homeless, which is good. Some give because they think I'm holy. Some want me to bless them; some want me to make them well."

"And what do you do with the money?"

"Selma Novik takes care of it. She is, how you say it, administrating since we let go secretary. We feed homeless, feed ourselves, and pay teachers."

"But they didn't give it to you to pay the teachers."

"They didn't say what for." He shrugged. "They just send money."

"And what do you do with the letters?"

"Send them receipt for soup."

"You mean recipe. Which brings me to why I came, Lev." I felt a little tweak in my heart as I began. "The Board wants to know what you have to do with the computer theft."

"Just a child's stunt, like stealing neighbor's plums. You didn't do that when you were a child?"

"This was more than plums. It was something like $20,000."

"It was more like finding money on street, or digging it up. Gold a peasant buried."

"You don't really believe that do you?" His responses were, as usual, ambiguous. Was he philosophizing, moralizing, condoning? As always it was hard for me to judge his words, even when I could find no fault in his conduct.

His eyes turned from whimsy to earnest and he said, "I read in papers about people who buy big business with company's own money, and ones who took over savings banks and steal hundreds of millions of dollars."

"What are you saying?"

"Only that this stunt would come as no surprise."

"Theft shouldn't come from a school with a religious sponsor. Some people are calling you a Fagan." I could see by his mild smile that he liked that reference to *Oliver Twist*. "It makes everybody look bad. This is, after all, not the ghetto. These kids have other choices."

"They didn't steal for themselves, Mendel. They were acting more like revolutionaries than crooks."

"That's no excuse." I swallowed the stone caught in my throat and threw him the punch line. "If you were part of it, the Board wants me to say that you must resign, or they'll give you the heave-ho."

He looked down and muttered, "Heave-ho." Then he stood up and went to the table, poured himself some tea while I waited in suspense, not knowing what he would say, but hoping that he had not been involved. He gestured to me with the teacup, his weary eyes mild and bemused.

"What does the Board want from me, to know if I told them to do it? The answer is no. Did they tell me what they were doing? No. Do I approve? No. Did money get spent for school? Yes."

I was relieved by his answer, not that I ever doubted it. "What about Karp and Bortz? Were they part of it? And who are "they"? Were there more than one of the kids involved?"

He went on to explain that the two old folks already had small annuities with the insurance company, and they were getting monthly checks. "Ask them yourself. From what I hear they were not to blame."

"You've looked into it."

"Of course. But you must talk to them too before government does what they do. What will they do, put them in prison?"

"I don't know." I got up and went towards him. He was looking out the window at the collection of old camping tents—yellow, green—where the homeless were now living.

"Have you seen food garden? You must see before you go. Five acres, all by hand. With elevated rows. When is done we can feed whole school, everybody."

"Who is working on it?"

"Many people. Mr. Harney, Hebrew teacher was *kibbutznick*. Maimonides Kravitz is learning French intensive cultivation method. Homeless take their turn. Children are learning botany, horticulture. Is very nice. Look down there and you will see a few of them with Harney. He is teaching gardening."

There was Harney, hoe in hand, watched by three weather-worn men and a toothless woman. Once again, I saw the good and I was glad.

"I'll look on the way out. For now, I must play detective."

I touched Lev's shoulder. He turned and looked at me with a smile that said, I know what you have to do and I don't blame you for it.

The computer hacker, Jonah Marabot, was in his room teasing his computer, or maybe talking with it. A tall boy, mostly arms and legs, with a long face and pale languid eyes—he was not what I had expected.

He stood and welcomed me without any sign of embarrassment or awkwardness, except that he didn't look me in the eye. It must have been feeding time for the computer. He slid a black wafer into its narrow mouth and listened as it chewed whatever was on it with clicking electronic teeth. The computer gratefully answered with a dazzling show of color in its cyclopean eye. Jonah looked pleased. I was intimidated.

"How fast does that thing go?" I asked, feeling dumb and wanting to open a dialogue.

Jonah mumbled something about giga seconds, adding that it was slow. "The latest chips perform 170 billion functions a second," he said in a flat voice, as if it was no big deal.

Imagine one of those little chips that make up a computer's mind can now go on and off 170 billion times in one second. Maybe it's a fake. After all, what could keep track of such a pace except another computer, which could also be lying. If there were a God in heaven, one capable of feeling pain and pleasure like people, it would surely be a little intimidated. For my part, I didn't know what to say, so I just gave a stupid nod.

I sat down on his bed and got him talking about his passion. Right off the bat he admitted that eavesdropping on other people's business was the reason he had been sent to our school. His father was a physicist at the University of Chicago and he, Jonah, had used their "Cray" to break into some "data" at the Department of Energy. It was information about reactor safety that hadn't been disclosed at some hearing, he explained, looking at a bunch of multicolored plastic pieces scattered on his desk.

"What did you do with the information?"

"I gave it to the newspapers," he replied, giving me a shy, mischievous look. "They, like, ate it up."

"What happened to you?"

"The newspaper attention took the pressure off of me, but I got sent here."

"How did you manage to get inside the insurance company's records?" For the second time that day I was in awe.

"A snap. I designed this program, like," and he went into some technical patois to tell me how he did it with the aid of something he called a modem. I looked around for the modem and couldn't see it. It did rhyme with Golem. I thought of the time Roe had used the insurance company computer and gotten the High Holiday seating all screwed up. This time the joke was on Roe.

"What made you do it?"

"Why do people climb rocks? It's what I do. Some people play the violin." He raised his head a little, as if to say everyone has their hobbies.

Then Jonah explained how he had gotten the idea. One day he distributed the mail—students take turns with some chores—and two envelopes from the local insurance company were addressed to Bortz and Kravitz. He watched them open them and find their annuity checks. So he thought, wouldn't it be interesting to add a couple of zeros to each of them. He expressed interest, examined the checks and convinced B and K to let him write down the numbers. They were suspicious at first but he assured them it was for a lottery he was entering. If he won he agreed to split the prize with them. They didn't buy this but went along with the story.

"I never ever even talked to them about what I was going to do, I swear it. They never knew who did it." He looked and sounded like he meant it. I wondered.

"How about Suzy Roe? Was she in on it?"

"Are you serious?"

The door to the room opened a little and I saw the blond, Slavic head of another student, Aryeh Jaffe, "Come on, Byte, or you'll miss Cross Country." His eyes shifted for an instant to take me in and he was gone. Aryeh's father was supposed to be an Israeli from Los Angeles who had a chain of car washes called the National Water Carrier. I understood that he'd been sent to our school after he had backed his father's Testosterosa, or whatever they called it, off the Santa Monica Pier.

Jonah stood up and danced from one foot to the other. I noticed he was wearing the same fancy inflatable sneakers that I'd seen on Bortz.

"Can I go now? Mr. Bron doesn't like us to be late."

"Have the authorities contacted you about the computer business?"

"No. Think they will?" he asked with prelapsarian innocence.

He didn't even wait for an answer. I heard the braying echoes of teenage laughter on the stairs. Moving around the humming computer, as I might avoid a chained and snarling Doberman, I left the scene of the crime and hunted for my next suspects knowing just where I would likely find them.

Bortz and Karp were hunched over a table in the dark corner of the faculty and old folks' lounge, wrapped in a cocoon of stale cigar smoke, eyes and ears focused on the rhythmic slap-slap of cards on the surface of the cigarette-scarred table.

"Hah! Gotcha!" rasped Karp and his head jerked up with a look of triumph.

His friend Bortz looked sour as he mentally calculated the toll. He opened both palms, bent his head to one side and said, "Nu! Over the last five years how many times have we exchanged the same ten bucks, tell me that?" and he looked my way for confirmation.

"He's right, Mendel," said Bortz. "But what pleasure. Nowadays only dreams give that kind of pleasure," he added with a lewd leer.

"Sit down and join us for a hand or two."

"Sorry, but I don't play cards."

"So we'll teach you," they said as a chorus.

"How's your running, Izzy?"

"I'm a new man! Here, feel my stomach. It's flat as a table."

"Thanks, I'll take your word." I pulled up a chair and they both turned toward me.

"If you want to know what we had to do with the checks, Mendel," said Gene, his bushy black eyebrows jumping up, "the answer is nothing."

"The checks came, and we figured we didn't need the money," said Karp.

"So why didn't you send the checks back?"

"What are you, the FBI?" Bortz

"No, but I suspect they'll be around."

"We didn't do nothing. Who are we to argue with the insurance company if they decide we're entitled to more money? After all, how many people pay attention."

"Besides, Mendel, the school got the money, except for my running shoes, and if the insurance company wants them they can have them back, and good luck." Karp again.

Both men looked righteously indignant. I backed off and their stern deeply wrinkled faces became boyish and mischievous.

"*Ganavim*," (thieves) I said, patting each of them on the shoulder.

"Bank error in our favor, Mendel. The pink card in the Monopoly set," said Gene Karp.

"Be sure you don't draw the one that says, Go to Jail, I retorted, glad to get away from the choking cigar smoke.

I wasn't Sam Spade or even Rumpole. My probing, if sympathetic, questions led me to conclude that nobody was really to blame, and nobody got much personal benefit. Besides, everybody knows insurance companies have plenty of money.

On my way to the car I went over to the garden, laid out in long rows of raised beds in what had once been a pasture. Nothing was growing yet but a lot of effort had gone into breaking and amending the soil with manure (I could smell it) and building the beds.

Harney, Maimonides Kravitz, and the same three homeless were going up the rows turning the soil, and they all stopped as I came up to watch. With his blue work shirt with the sleeves rolled to his muscular biceps, his faded work-worn jeans, and a battered straw hat, Harney, red-faced and sweating, looked like someone who might have spent a decade in the same field. In contrast, Mi Kravitz, with his rumpled beige cotton coat, old white shirt and his ever-present multi-colored *keepah*, looked more like a gardener of the mind. The homeless seemed to have stepped out of the pages of a Dorothea Lange photo essay of the Dust Bowl, except that there was fresh hope in their rheumy eyes.

"Mendel," said Mi Kravitz. "Here, take a hoe and chop a little dirt. It's good for the soul, you know," and he thrust the weathered shaft of his hoe toward me.

I took it and made a few tentative dents in the soil of one of the raised beds. It was yielding and gave off a fresh organic smell.

Harney introduced me to the others, who offered rough, calloused workmen's hands and shy smiles.

"We're just about to plant carrots."

I handed the hoe back to Mi and excused myself, as I had to get back to the synagogue for a meeting of the budget committee. But it would have been nice all the same. My grandfather had been an able gardener. I still recall the sweet taste of his tomatoes.

Kravitz shouldered his hoe like a rifle and walked with me to my car. "So, Mendel. Will we survive the trouble?"

"I'll do what I can, Mi."

"It would be a shame if it all fell apart, you know. Every one of us out here feels as if we've been reborn. We were just passing time before the school came. And now," he raised his hoe skyward, "I feel like Faust reclaiming the swamps."

"And what about the computer theft? Do you have any opinion?"

"I've never paid much attention to money matters, never even balanced a checkbook. But for me it's just a prank." I opened the car door and sat down. Mi kept me from closing it as he said, "One thing more. Don't let them hurt Lev. I know he goes his own way, but that's his strength. He reminds me, more than a little, of the Baal Shem Tov, you know. He is a righteous man." He held me in his gaze, intense with conviction before he closed my car door and turned away, walking a little stiffly, his out of place black oxford shoes covered with mud.

"Mi!" I called after him. "I'll do what I can." He responded by raising his hoe over his head. He walked back toward the garden with his rolling flat-footed gait, singing the chorus of an old Spanish Civil War song, "*Wir sind die Moorsoldaten.*"

I drove out of the grounds of the school feeling both heavy and light. There were the problems to be faced but there was also a rare hopeful spirit, the excitement of being part of something new that seemed to have possessed everyone in different ways.

# TWENTY-THREE

# A Close Shave

I went home and warmed up a bagel before calling Nudelman. He sounded a little remote and abrupt but maybe it
was because he was at the office. After I finished my report
there was a long silence and I could imagine him at his desk,
his eyes ranging over a contract or a sale report.

"So what would you do?" he finally asked me.

"Do? I would defend Lev against all of his detractors and
keep the school going."

"Even if we lose the case and have to give it up?"

"Yes. If I could I would."

"Thanks." I heard him talking to someone in his office
before he said, "I gotta get off the phone. See you tonight at
the Board meeting. Bring your six-gun."

I dropped in at the budget committee but didn't have the
energy to respond too many of the questions and Rabbi Bing
looked up out of the depths of his glasses with unusual disapproval, but what could I do? I was obsessed with the school.

As soon as I could I bolted the meeting and buried my head in my books. Sinking into my armchair, calmed by a Motrin, I spent the rest of the day reading *Tales of the Hassidim,* by Martin Buber although maybe it should have been the New Testament.

I dined alone on Campbell's chicken noodle soup then, girding my loins—Isn't that what warriors do before battle? I went upstairs to the synagogue boardroom to face the whole crowd. Why should I feel so tense? Had I absorbed into my very pores all of the uncertainty and trouble of the school as if I had done it all, the good and the bad? This was too much. Maybe I need to see a shrink.

So let me get to the point. I gave my report, telling them what I told Nudelman. The reaction? Frowns, some sour lips, a few nods, a couple of assenting smiles, and a look of encouragement from Nudelman.

Rosenzweig was next, still fighting the battle of the bulge, his drooping cheeks making him look even more like a bloodhound than before his weight loss. Roe moved his chair away as Rosenzweig pulled out one of his 50-caliber cigars and lit it.

I don't know whether it was the smoke or the way he put things, but everybody was confused when he had finished. Maybe it's the complexity of the law, which seems to be a process of forever seeking but not finding resolution, much like the search for happiness. "True", he said, we had lost two rounds in the suit brought by the Mossberg family to break the trust. True we no longer could use the money, but the case was not yet over. He and his law clerks were preparing an exhaustive brief to prove that the school was compatible with the trust intent. All the old folks had given their declarations to prove it, and the feeding of the homeless was actually in our favor, since it was a purely charitable function not unlike curing people and so on.

"Enough!" shouted Finkelstein, butting in as he often did. "This is a circus!" He brandished his fist like a sword and cleared his throat. "We open a school and find ourselves investigated by the FBI, at war with the Immigration Service, in court to keep the trust, harboring a false messiah, aiding and abetting the PLO. Is this a nice little small town religious community, I ask you, or a multinational corporation? Next thing you know we'll have to can the teachers and hire a battalion of lawyers."

"What's your point?" asked Nudelman.

"We must get rid of Lev. Drop the defense. Let the government send him back to Russia."

"Is that a motion?" His voice was steady and unemotional, but his ears were on fire.

"Yes. It's a motion."

Discussion ensued. That's what I wrote in the minutes but what an understatement. I won't repeat it. There are, after all, no Ciceros among us, but there was plenty of passion, logic, and illogic. After two hours, a vote: a tie—three to terminate Lev and let him be deported; three to keep him.

It was up to Nudelman. Most of the heads turned his way although Roe was drawing an elaborate Star of David on the notepad in front of him. I never thought of Nudelman as being at all dramatic, but he certainly made the best of that silent extended moment before he said in a matter-of-fact tone, "Against."

A murmur of approval and disapproval went around the table. Rosenzweig broke open a bag of M&Ms and scooped a handful into his mouth. I was glad, relieved. We had come down on the right side for now. How long we would go on was another question. Poor Lev didn't know it but he was walking the stakes of a picket fence.

# TWENTY-FOUR

# Heart's Counsel

The day after the Board meeting I had to go to Pittsburgh— a little get away—for a few hours in the library to work on my early Jewish settler's piece, and to browse in a bookstore or two. I found an out-of-print book on the Khazars. Next came a little pasta, a friend, and finally a good orchestra seat at the symphony. Perelman was the soloist. A day like this is a month to me, away from the telephone, the bills, and the constant little favors that everybody expects of a minor official. Who needs a cruise in the Caribbean or a condo on the water when a change of scenery, some anonymity, and a few things you really like are so easy to come by?

Besides, there was the company of an old acquaintance to look forward to, Leopoldo Mazzini, a shoemaker from Milan whom I had met at a concert many years back. A man with hands as hard as the sole of a shoe, a gladiator's nose, and a passion for music. To see him in his tiny shop in his blue work apron you would think he had nothing to say, but the music, always in the background, gave a hint of more.

Beyond a common appreciation of good music, Leopoldo and I shared something deeper: the notion that, but for circumstances, our lives might have been less obscure. Of course I had my writing, which no one except Estelle ever saw, and he composed sonatas played on the piano to a condescending gathering of cousins on his birthday. Who can say, that may be all anyone needs, but that question is not what I wanted to deal with.

What is important about this particular day was what happened that afternoon not far from Kaufman's Department Store. I had some time to kill and having seen a sale advertised in the window I decided to buy a couple of dress shirts; they had been marked down forty-five percent. Estelle was always telling me that my collars were too long. I left the store having pawed through a pile of shirts and actually found one my size.

I was waiting at a crosswalk when I saw, or thought I saw, Estelle and Lev Kyol walking through the brass and glass doors of an art deco office building. The building was down and across the street from where I was standing, and I had seen them from the back. Had it been only Lev, I might not have been so certain. The two together were easy to identify. Lev was so tall and bony. As for Estelle, I would have recognized her even before I could see her features.

My first reaction was surprise followed by curiosity bordering on suspicion. Here was another dimension to their relationship, more than giving him dinner, confiding, ironing his shirts. Now Estelle, my Estelle, was spending time with him, in Pittsburgh no less.

The light changed, and I elbowed my way through the crowd and hustled to the building, but by the time I got inside they had disappeared up one of the eight elevators. Vainly, I looked at the building directory for a clue to their intent but there was just about everything: lawyers, doctors, jewelers, insurance agencies, investment consultants, travel agents, even a hat store and an art gallery. The building was the three-dimensional realization of the yellow pages.

The mystery hung an alienating cloud over the rest of my carefree day. Of course, dinner with my friend in his cousin's restaurant was pleasant. We even split a bottle of some obscure Italian red wine—it wasn't Chianti. We made an odd-looking pair: Leo in his loose black velvet jacket smelling faintly of shoe polish, looking like a cartoon of a maestro, and me in my frumpy brown tweed jacket with the too-narrow lapels offset by the too-wide shirt collar.

"You're not yourself, Mendel." He asked me over the tiramisu and espresso. "You're usually so loquacious," he added, with his rolling Italian accent that struck each syllable.

With that invitation I bared my soul, as they say in cheap romances. After all, who better to talk about such things than with a music-loving Italian?

He looked at me with those wise black eyes and said, "You make too much of it, and anyhow, you've been talking about this Estelle for years and you have had lots of opportunity to develop the romantic side of your relationship." He raised his finger and shook it like a conductor chastising the violin section. "But you have not done so, for what reason—a lack of courage, timidity? If you have missed your opportunity, be philosophical; it is your own doing. You are too old to play the heartsick Romeo. You are not married so the cuckold role doesn't fit you either. And you wouldn't make a Don Juan."

"What should I do?"

"If it is not too late, fight for her."

I'd been told. I had no right to feel sorry for myself. I must be affirmative, declare myself. After all, I'd managed with Sarah Cavanaugh and I had my widow in McKeesport. True, I had started slowly with Sarah, but once I knew the lay of the land I wasn't one to hold back. I drank the rest of my coffee while Leo watched over me with sympathy.

"I forget which concerto we are to hear, the Brahms or the Mendelsohn," I said.

"Neither. It's Beethoven."

"Beethoven."

His words still stung.

TWENTY-FIVE

# Late Love Early

What a dream I had that night! I had to catch a plane and I was late. All kinds of things happened. My car wouldn't start, which is not such a fantasy. I had to push it myself uphill to get it started. There was endless traffic and cars cutting me off. Suddenly I was at the airport waiting for a ticket with the line going nowhere. I was running with a departure sign blinking in my head, running down a long endless corridor, which was now empty, running and knowing why it was empty. The plane had already left. But there was no end in sight. I woke up, my heart pounding. The red numbers on the clock said 3:19. I drank a glass of milk and went back to bed, but the dream remained stamped in my mind like a larger-than-life billboard.

All right, it wasn't much of a dream and not at all obscure. I'm not Freud or Bruno Shultz but the meaning was obvious. I had missed Estelle. Under this lesson was yet another, more important, realization. I wanted Estelle for myself, not just as a person to confide in but more, much more.

I sorted my thoughts like washed laundry arranged in little piles. First there was the love pile with one sock missing for it lacked the urgent passion of youth. Yet in a quiet way I wanted her. Yes, she stirred me. I liked to touch her, liked to be next to her, liked to smell that cherry coke perfume and observe her small gestures; the way she raised her gull wing eyebrows when she was troubled, the quick way she moved her forefinger when she was making a point, the tears in her eyes when she thought of something sentimental.

Was she the only woman I ever wanted? No. Could I live without her? Surely. Would her being bound to another man leave a great emptiness in my soul, a loss? Yes. Yes. Oh, yes. That was the realization. I had taken her for granted, moving in my slow way, always intimidated by the presence of her dead husband, putting off and putting off the moment when our affection might turn physical, until the door was closing in my face.

Given my state of mind, what was I to do about it? By this time, grey was seeping into the Eastern horizon giving form to the tree outside my bedroom window. There were weeds growing in my head from my sleepless, irresolute night and I opened the window and let the chill, damp morning air towel me awake. The air that met me was as fresh as the morning itself and already wearing the honey spice scent of hyacinths.

I made strong coffee and thought about what might be done, if anything, to save my eroding chance to have Estelle. Should I call her? No. More intimacy, eye contact, would be needed. Why do people spend so much time talking on the phone? Do they want to be insulated from closeness, make their contact more abstract, more electronic? This was no time for that question.

I resolved to go see her, but when? Now. She was an early riser and seldom left home before ten. Besides, if I went now, I might catch the two of them together, but did I want to? And what would I do if I saw them sitting, cozy and familiar, at the breakfast table, she refilling his coffee cup while he reads *Pravda*? Ha, ha, a mad thought borne of distorted jealousy. But still, what if? How should I act? What should I say? Bow out? Apologize for butting in?

I dressed and rushed over, probably going through at least one stop sign. I hadn't a clue what I would say when I got there. Let it come out, whatever happened to reach my tongue from my heart as I walked up to the door, hardly aware of the newly planted screaming pansies, and rattled the brass knocker, the one with the menacing lion's face.

My ears felt like they would pop as I waited for the door to open. There she was, looking out through the crack, her face unmade, showing a spark of curiosity and, I was glad to see, welcome in her eyes.

"Mendel. What a surprise. It's barely eight o'clock." She stood in the door in her robe, silky with a Japanese floral pattern in rose shades, the lacy top of her nightgown showing. I looked over her shoulder, half-expecting to see an unshaven Lev skittering for cover.

"May I come in?"

"Of course. Why ask? Have I ever turned you away?"

I advanced cautiously, like a soldier crossing no man's land. "I thought you might be occupied."

"I was just making some dough for a cake. The bridge club is coming this afternoon. And I was thinking about going to the nursery and buying some vegetable sets. The garden at the school has inspired me. You've seen it?"

"Yes."

"Isn't it marvelous?"

"It's quite a garden."

We had reached the kitchen and I looked around for signs of another person, a second coffee cup. To my relief there was just one cup on the maple table, a half-eaten piece of toast and the newspaper, open to those inscrutable stock market listings.

"So, how's the market?"

"Down 24, but you're not really interested, Mendel."

I sat down, waited as she poured me a cup of coffee and looked out the window toward the back of the garden. Sure enough, the old vegetable patch had been weeded and two furrows were freshly turned.

"Who did that?" I asked, pointing.

"I did." She raised an arm and flexed her muscle. "The aerobics are doing wonders for me."

"Everybody's getting fit." My stomach began to push at my belt and I wondered if I should do more for my body. More? Why not something? I had given up the jogging.

She poured some coffee for herself and sat down across from me, her eye's ranging down the stock columns, very domestic, very appealing. What if we did this every morning? I would do the crossword, she would translate the stock market. We would chat about the Far East, the Middle East, whether we should take in the latest play in Pittsburgh, invite the Nudelmans to dinner, take a trip. Was I up to it after my long, solitary life with nobody to talk to in the morning but my choice of a thousand writers and philosophers, all of them dead? But I was getting ahead of myself; she had already made a choice, one that I had to undo.

"So, how's Lev?"

"Why do you ask?" she said without looking up, but her voice sounded more alert.

"You see a lot of him," I thrust.

"So do you," she parried.

"But in a different way."

"How different, Mendel?"

"He confides in you."

"He tells me he respects you more than anyone," she said, finally looking at me with that keen, what's-on-your-mind look.

"He does? That's nice. I think he's great, if a little foolhardy."

"He's got a rare courage, one that comes from—" She stopped short of what might have been an insight or a revelation. She remembered her dough and got up to knead it. The yeasty smell escaped from the yellow ceramic bowl and brought back memories of the kitchen of my childhood. She hovered over the bowl, her body moving to the rhythm of her hands. It was very sensual.

"What were you doing with him in Pittsburgh yesterday?" I asked this suddenly, aware that it was untimely.

She looked up from the dough, irritated, quizzical. "Why do you ask? For that matter, how do you know?"

"I saw you both going into a building."

Her face showed unspoken assent and she waited for me to say more.

"Estelle, I thought we were close."

"We are close. What's bothering you about my spending the day with Lev?"

"You're right, I shouldn't be bothered. I'm not bothered," I protested. "Just curious."

"Curiosity killed the cat."

"Now you're being cute."

"Are you jealous?" she asked with a coy look.

"No, no, not exactly."

"You have no right to be, after all."

"I know that. I have no claim on you."

"The claim of friendship. But no monopoly."

I was ready to give up. She had chased me round the barn twice, like a cat after a mouse. I might as well just ask the question, I thought. "Is there something special going on with you and Lev?"

"Mendel, aren't you getting personal?"

"Yes, as a matter of fact. I feel, have felt for a long time, that you're keeping something from me."

"And if I am?"

"Estelle, let's stop the badger."

"You mean banter."

"I had the fantasy that you were going to a jeweler to buy an engagement ring or whatever."

This made her laugh. "Why should it matter to you, Mendel? If we were, I'm sure you'd be the first to congratulate me."

"No, I wouldn't, not inside.

"Why not?"

"Because…because I had someday hoped…that we would be more than close friends." She watched me with earnest attention. "That one day we would be intimate. But I wanted to wait until Sidney's cigar smoke left the drapes, so to speak."

"Sidney's been gone for years."

"I guess I'm slow."

"Mendel, a eunuch would have moved faster." She shook her head in a bemused way and looked at me with tenderness.

"And now it's too late?"

"I have an appointment at the hairdresser, if you're thinking about this morning."

"Estelle."

"Mendel?"

"I guess I should go."

She touched my arm and said, "Why did you wait all this time."

"I really don't know."

"Well, I want you to know that I'm touched." And she kissed me, lightly on the lips, and shooed me out of the house.

I walked to the car feeling like an incomplete sentence. Maybe I should get a dog, I thought.

## TWENTY-SIX

# Knowing the Trees

That afternoon I got a call from Lev; an unusual call. He didn't like to use the telephone, a carryover from his years in the Soviet Union when phones were alternately tapped or broken. "When it's working you know they are listening," he once told me with one of his wry smiles. I was surprised when he asked me to come, pick him up and take him for a stroll in the country. "It's time of year and I miss it. I am too much in my bureau," he explained.

Considering my fit of jealousy and my inconclusive exit from Estelle's house, I felt awkward but still compelled to spend a few hours with him; even share one of my commonplace walks. I was sure he would like it, for nature to the Russians doesn't have to be framed in gigantic mountains. They seem to enjoy finding an edible mushroom or a wild berry in the knee of a tree root—so my reading tells me.

He was waiting for me on a bench, his blue shirt open at the neck, a little flush on his broad forehead daubed by the bright spring sun. He must have been dozing for he opened his eyes and didn't seem to recognize me. Immediately he nodded a little wearily and unfolded his long frame from the bench.

We drove to my shaded creek deep in its crease of the earth and parked the car near the wooden bridge. The water somersaulted and leaped over worn mossy rocks and here and there a spear of sunlight probed its skin and made a dazzling wound. The leaf overhead was still spring fresh and translucent green. I had brought a snack: two ripe bananas, a Coke for him, and some apple juice for me. He was fascinated with bananas, and had taken to Coke, perhaps to ingratiate himself with the children although for me it was too sweet—but Russians put sugar in everything, even soup.

There we were side by side feeling the damp of the earth creeping through our pants. Lev was peeling and munching, peeling and munching, nursing from the Coke and occasionally humming to himself what sounded like a Russian folk song.

"I cannot get used to abundance," he finally said, as if he were finishing a thought begun in his head. "And with it all I cannot get used to poor, to crime, to indifference of one to other, to…fixations that seize like epidemic, seize everybody: Congress, plain people, so-called media. It is interesting word, 'media.' What does it mean, I wonder."

His thoughts had wandered across the landscape of our national personality, finally alighting like a fly on our national conscience.

"What do you think it means?" I asked, standing, dusting off my seat and giving him my hand. His hand was warm and damp, as if he'd been sweating. Men shake hands with each other, testing their strength, bonding and depending and trusting for an instant. An old habit from a time when a hand that held no weapon was not feared. But now our hands, his and mine, had bonded in a different way, to lift one up with the strength of the other. This was more than a handshake.

"I looked up media in *slovar*." He had used the Russian word for dictionary. "It is membrane of artery. Also, it is soft mute sound. Do not you think that defines all mess communication? A screwy language, English. You can say that, 'screwy'?"

"Yes, although it makes no sense." We walked up the rutted track between the banks, arched over by long maple limbs. It seemed as if the trees were reaching out to touch each other. A bird suddenly sang out, a jazz improvisation.

"I know that song," he said. "I heard it in forest around Moscow. Why do birds speak same halfway around world?" It was not really a question.

He blinked as we came out of the hollow into the bright sun. Fields rolling like the patches on a down quilt, stitched together and separated at the same time by wire fences or rows of trees, stretched to the horizon that rose toward a downy blue and white sky. In the nearest field, a grey tractor was breaking the dark soil and the yielding ground rose to the plow like the wake of a boat.

"Good soil," he said.

"You never married?" I asked.

"No."

"Did you ever want to?"

"I had girl I loved once. But she married another. She was engineer; she married another engineer. They move to Kiev. Later I love teacher at my school. For many years we were together but she didn't want to marry. No place to live. Not very good reason but I had to accept it. So we are same, you and me."

Yes, I thought, we are the same: middle-aged and seeking the same woman. The two sides of my brain had a little argument over my next questions. Should I mention Estelle or not? I was in the middle of this debate when Lev started to fall to the ground. My first thought was that he had stumbled, and I grabbed his arm to hold him but he continued to drop and I realized that the life had gone out of him. I grabbed him with my other hand and did my best to ease him down, watching that his head, limp on his neck, didn't strike a rock. I dropped to my knees beside him and cradled the back of his head in my hand.

"Lev," I said with urgency as I searched my mind to recall the steps of CPR. His face was bloodless, and he was out. Was it a stroke? His breathing was regular at least. We were alone. There was no house in sight. I couldn't leave him to run for help and I couldn't risk picking him up, even if I could carry him. I picked up his limp hand and began to rub it. I patted his cheek and pulled back his eyelid to see if his pupil was dilated. A sign of a brain injury, I thought. He was still unconscious, and I began to feel a flood of panic in my chest when, to my relief, his hand began to flex, and he turned his head. He opened his eyes, but they saw nothing. He looked confused at first and didn't seem to know me, and then awareness returned with the color to his cheeks. He started to sit up, but I held him back.

"Wait, rest just a moment."

"I must have tripped and hit my head. I'm alright now."

"Do you hurt anyplace?"

"No."

I helped him to his feet. He seemed steady enough.

"Do you want to sit down?" With this, any thought of confronting him over Estelle evaporated.

"No. We must walk on. It is so beautiful and quiet." We had come to a farmhouse, two stories, once white and now grey, with a pitched shingle roof and a wide porch. A dog, a longhaired brown and white shepherd, ran out to the road to inspect us and greet us with several stifled barks. Behind the house a woman was pinning white sheets to a clothesline.

"Have you read Tolstoy? He idolizes peasant. Are farmers here like Tolstoy's peasants?"

"Hardly. Here they must be economists to survive."

We walked in silence again. Slightly round shouldered, he looked like he was enjoying himself. He had recovered fully from his fall. I thought of the latest articles in the newspaper about him. The notion that he was Christ returned to earth seemed to have died down, largely because he had done nothing at all to encourage it, avoiding interviews, refusing offers to speak. He had nothing more to say, he claimed, and his duties at the school kept him from leaving.

Even so, according to Morley Rasmussen, a handful of people, Pentecostals, were going on without him. He was the second coming. Morley thought they were "wacky" but totally sincere in their belief. Elmo was still preaching during the open hour at the Pentecostal church and, rumor had it, had been invited to several other churches in other states.

"What's happening with the people who think you are the Messiah?"

"I neither encourage nor discourage them in their beliefs."

A line of electric pylons crossed the road and marched up a hill carrying drooping wires on their outstretched arms. A dozen or so birds were perched on the wires.

"I have often wondered if birds are aware that they sit on so much electricity in wires," he said, gesturing at the birds.

Was this digression or parable, I wondered. To a bird, a wire coursing with power was just a place to rest. Was he trying to say that there might be more to him as well?

"Isn't your ambiguity a kind of false prophesy?"

"Think about it, my friend. What if Jesus was just man of flesh and blood, leader of men, breaker of images and conventions?"

"Which is what we Jews believe."

"Yes, but what if he was also something more? What if he was truly righteous man, a *lamed he*, in our own mythology; a man whose purity fused in him great, positive force of nature, the life force if you will, God. Let us say he was, what is word, personification of life force. What then was he? Just man? Or more than man?" He swung his arms and flailed the air for emphasis and his tone was both calm and intense, as if he were sharing more than random conversation on a country walk.

"Yes, I see what you mean. But you—"

"Me? I will not judge myself. It is for others to judge me, to take my measure."

I mentally chewed on what he had said. The messiah was metaphor, poetry, and yet real as well. There could be, would be, many messiahs, some recognized and registered by those who believed, others passing like the wind but leaving no less a footprint on the trace of life.

"I am a little tired. Maybe we turn back?" he said. "The next time we go over next hill and see what we see. As boy I always wanted to do that, you too?"

"Yes. It is human to be curious."

"Not just curious. Hopeful. If what we might see would be repulsive or fearful, we wouldn't rush on to see it. It is hope that what we see will give us pleasure that keeps us going, over next hill. I think."

Again, silence as we trudged back on our steps, breathing the sweet breath of new life.

"Mendel, I must confess something."

"What?" I expected him to reveal that he and Estelle were getting married.

"Some publishing house wants me to write book about my old life, what I do, did when I come here. Amazing."

"You are becoming a bit of a celebrity, Lev. In fact, you've taken off like a Mars probe."

"Oh, I have done nothing special in my life."

"You're not going to turn it down?" I was envious, I must say. Nobody had ever come to me to publish my scribblings.

"I'm not going to do it. I'm sure."

"But why?"

"No time, even if I had something to say. Too busy."

My admiration for him went up a couple of notches. He was so humble and modest. I almost forgave him for taking my Estelle. He deserved her and needed her, maybe even more than I did.

TWENTY-SEVEN

# False Witness

Our walk in the country was an intermission, one of those savored quiet moments during a time of prolonged stress, a battle with a sickness, a bitter divorce, a time when hope is replenished. I left Lev without bitterness, without having confronted him with his connection to Estelle. After all, what right did I have? I felt stupid, and Lev had enough troubles—how much I wasn't yet aware of. I could have put two and two together had I stepped away from my own emotional tangle and looked clearly at his life.

Walking down the street or sitting on a bus I am always awed by the fact that the woman pushing the shopping cart on my right, the man in the pin-striped suit carrying the leather briefcase on my left, the Japanese man with black straight hair sticking out from under a Pirates baseball cap—each represents a complex and unique universe of memory and experience, different from mine, different from everyone, isolated by their own being and experience, yet bumping into me, with as little as a friendly glance or as much as a shared life. Our contacts are so different in their quality and duration, sharing or exposing so little of the stored whole. In the end, what we feel and share and communicate is such a tiny fragment of what we are.

I am locked in a lifetime of isolation, a prisoner of the limits of my body. What I know is restricted to what I can pick up with my senses and read with my imagination. I walk with Lev, talk with him, and hear a small, distorted message out of the whole, a crackly signal from a cheap shortwave radio beamed from the other side of the world, an SOS or a birthday card. I touch Estelle's shoulder and feel, or think I feel, the vibration of her soul—maybe it is my own soul. I look into her eyes and think I see understanding, affection, anger—maybe it is all my projection, but it is never more than a nearsighted view into the unwashed window of another's home.

"What's new about that? Everybody knows it. Nothing original. Even so it needs to be said once-in-a-while, especially when we think sometimes that we know all about this and that. We never do.

I was sitting at my desk, actually an old table that I bought for thirty-five dollars when they closed the only branch of the county library. No money in the budget, besides the only people using it were people who just wanted to get out of the cold or the rain, so the report said. You've heard that before, too. Don't get the idea I'm in a gloomy mood.

The phone rang. It was Nudelman. Would I go to the school right away? He would have gone but he had to go to Youngstown. "An important meeting that I can't get out of," he apologized.

Nudelman, you go to the school; it's your school, and I'll go to the meeting in Youngstown, I thought. It was, after all, your creation. I didn't say that. "What's up?" I said that.

"FBI."

"What?"

"A couple of agents are out there wanting to talk to people, see records, who knows? I called Rosenzweig but he's out of town."

"Nudelman, what do I know from the FBI?"

"Just go and look. Be cooperative. I've got to go, Mendel. I'm late. Sorry to dump this on you."

"OK, Nudelman, you'll owe me one."

"More than one, Mendel. Bye."

I hadn't even had breakfast. Shaking my head and mumbling to myself, I sprayed some raisin bran into a bowl, splashed some milk over it, and crunched it down, not tasting anything. What was I to do with the FBI? What if they wanted to take Lev away; put him on the next flight to Moscow from Pittsburgh International? Did they have a flight from Pittsburgh to Moscow? I had no idea. On one level that thought produced a little champagne bubble in my heart—until my conscience burst it. I fortified myself with coffee, took a shower, and then went into battle.

They were sitting across from Selma Novik in the lounge. She had already bribed them with coffee and her famous tea cakes. I approached them trying to put a mask of stolid confidence over my apprehension. Not that I equated the FBI with the Gestapo, but I had read about some underhanded tricks played against the Anti-War Movement, and I was on my guard.

Selma greeted me with the air of a grand dame who was entertaining a few acquaintances at her country house for the weekend.

The two men stood, faced me with the same earnest, sober look—they must have learned it in FBI school—and flapped open their leather wallets. They had licenses to be FBI agents, pictures and everything. I inspected the documents. They seemed surprised at this but what did I know about F. B. I. convention. They looked at me. I looked at them.

They both looked like they had once been college athletes. They were neatly dressed: their ties choked up to the top, their shoes shined—good stout walking shoes too, good boys. Was the bulge behind their jackets a shoulder holster concealing a gun? What for? Did this look like a money laundry or a cocaine laboratory? Who knows where they are going next. Anyhow, Martucci was the older. He had the face of a Roman: a bumpy, broad bridged nose, one that could be stuck in the crack of a door and not get mashed. Who did he look like… Ah, Lee Iacocca, the Chrysler salesman. Only Martucci didn't have the big smile.

The younger one, Shaw, was Afro-American, a good-looking guy with a strong jaw, one that wouldn't break on contact with a fist. My hand stung from the squeezing it got. You can always tell something from the way people shake hands. What, I don't know.

"Both of these gentlemen are lawyers, Mendel," said Selma with a touch of surprise.

"Rosenzweig, the school lawyer, couldn't be here," I said with an apology.

"They are here about the insurance checks," said Selma. She was sitting straight in her chair wearing a faded floral cotton dress, her hands folded in her lap. "I told them it was just a school boy's prank." They both smiled at that.

"Where's Mi?" I asked. Knowing him, I was sure that he would want to sit in.

"It's his day to work in the office. He and I take turns, you know." She looked very proud of herself. Over the months, Selma and Maimonides had come to think of the school as their family. Not only were they doing much of the administrative and office work, they were even sitting in on some of the faculty committees.

"We need to talk to..." Martucci looked at the page of his little notebook and read out the names, mispronouncing most of them in a raspy voice. "We've been waiting for someone who represents the board of directors before we begin."

"Then you haven't come to take anybody away?"

"We're just here to get some information, that's all," said Shaw.

They talked to each other quietly and Martucci went off to see Schweig. Sami Arakat was loitering in the hall outside the door.

"Since you have nothing else to do, Sami," I said, "kindly find Mr. Bortz and Mr. Karp." By the look of him, the word was out that the FBI was paying a visit. He trotted off.

While we waited, Shaw complimented Selma on her tea cakes and she dictated the recipe, which he wrote down in his notebook. I wondered whether it would become evidence in the case. He was nice, although he kept asking questions—how did a retirement home become a school? and things like that.

He told us about his mother who lived in Newark, New Jersey, and her favorite recipes for biscuits, and Shaw and Selma got into a discussion over the essential ingredients. Selma liked to add a dollop of sour cream. Shaw only liked them with sweet cream. Selma was recalling the best one she had ever eaten, at a hotel in Tennessee, on a vacation back before the war—which war she didn't specify—when Bortz and Kravitz came in, looking scared.

Shaw took them in as he would two second cousins at a family reunion. They told him the same thing they had told me. By the look of him he was more amused than disturbed. He looked down at those air-filled running shoes and said, "My brother has a pair of those. They make you go faster?"

"Well, at my age, you know…" said Karp and that was it. No more questions. Bortz and Karp went off to play, looking relieved.

"You have a way of putting people at their ease, Mr. Shaw," I said.

"You can catch more flies with honey," said Selma. "You know they didn't mean any harm. It was like found money to them. And it all went to the school. I know; I handle the finances." Shaw was listening. I was getting nervous.

Shaw was telling Selma about his four brothers and two sisters when Martucci came back, looking like the home team had just been upset. Apparently, Schweig had given him an earful. I wish I could have been there.

Next, he wanted to talk to Jonah Marabot, "the hacker."

"I'm afraid he's not here," said Selma.

"Where is he?"

"His father came to get him. They live in Chicago, you know. I spoke with him. So did Maimonides. The director was out of town. The boy's father said he will pay the insurance company for their loss."

"Yes. We already know that".

"Would you like another tea cake?"

"No, thank you, ma'am."

"I can send some home with you."

"No, thanks, but we would like to see the director before we leave."

"I'll take you to his office," I volunteered, eager to get them away from Selma before she said too much.

Once in the hall, I asked, "What did Schweig have to say?"

"I'm afraid I can't tell you that."

"Whatever it was, you should take it with a grain of salt." I quickly explained the state of hostility between Schweig and everybody else around the school.

"We are aware of his role," said Martucci. This took us to the closed door of Lev's office. I knocked, softly, hoping he was away, any place but at Estelle's house. Unfortunately, I heard his voice and we entered to find him, as usual, at his desk.

"The FBI," I announced, and he stood up and looked at them without any surprise or apprehension. He looked worn, cadaverous, even more so than a few days ago. Tension and a lack of sleep had painted dark lines under his eyes. Before he could ask I said, "We've just had tea with Selma."

Again the questions, but these dealt more with his work in Russia. He answered directly, simply, and without hesitation, telling them what he had told me. No surprises. Then they got into the computer business. He answered the first few questions in the same way, then he raised both of his hands like a surrendering soldier and said, "I want you to know before you go any further that I accept full blame for what happened."

After all of his denials I was both stunned and afraid for him. He was issuing his own ticket back to Russia even if all the money was paid back. But in line with his confession I must make my own. I was relieved to think that if he had to leave, it would be alone.

Martucci and Shaw looked at each other. "I guess we should give you the Miranda warning," Martucci said, and he rattled off something about holding his words against him.

"I am sure that is true. I know it from Soviet Union," Lev responded with a tired little smile.

"What is the extent of your involvement?"

"Total, from beginning. I convinced boy to do it for school, you understand, not for me, for school."

"What made you think of it?"

"I read about what he had done in a letter with his application. Later, when we needed money, it came to me."

The more he said the less convinced I was that he had been part of it. He was making it up, taking the rap as they said in the old George Raft movies. What for?

I could have said something then—interrupted, interceded, or told them it wasn't true—but I didn't. I just sat there and watched and listened, wondering how it would come out.

There are many things we do in life that we regret. Some are just dumb errors, lapses of attention, like a fender bender or locking the keys in the house. These we forget the next day. But not coming to Lev's aid, buying Estelle with my silence, I will always regret. Many times since, I have spoken silently the words I did not say. And I came to the conclusion that the Miranda warning was only half of the truth. The words you do not say will also be held against you.

# TWENTY-EIGHT

# The Price of Sparrows

I finally got through to Nudelman. He sounded tired on the phone but asked me to come over after dinner. Hunched over a pile of papers in his cluttered home office, he looked every bit as weary as he had sounded. Sprawled at his feet on the rug, Mandy lifted her flat head and thumped her tail as I sat down.

Nudelman's reaction was less enthusiastic. He gave a deep sigh, and said, "Excuse me for being so abrupt on the phone, Mendel. I've just been through a ball-breaking negotiation with the owners of a truck dealership in Youngstown that's going down the tubes."

"So how did you do?"

"We may have made a deal but it's going to be tough."

"All the best, Nudelman."

"So, what's with the FBI?" he asked, putting his hands behind his head. I told him the story and watched as his face went from weary to concerned and finally disgusted. It's amazing how small changes in features communicate different states of mind in the human face. We have all these special muscles for communication, in contrast to a dog, for example, that can only narrow its eyes, pull its lips back and show its teeth, or wag its tail.

"Why in hell did he do that to himself?" he asked with the sharp pitch of despair in his voice. "When he said before that it wasn't his doing, I believed him, didn't you?"

"I still do. He wouldn't do such a thing. I know it. It's below him."

Nudelman was fussing with his pipe, stuffing some of that tobacco into it that smelled of honey before it was burned.

Mandy snapped at a fly then dropped her head on her paws. A sudden chill gust came in through the half-open window and the sky growled in the distance.

"Rain," Nudelman said as his teeth clicked down on his pipe stem. He pulled on the pipe, let the smoke leak out of his mouth, and watched as the wind dispersed it, then said in a smoky voice, "I'm afraid we'll have to go back to the Board." He turned toward the window and watched as the fat blue clouds moved toward us. "All I wanted was a good education for Isaac, something you'd think we could have gotten from the Monogonessen School District," he said more to himself than to me.

"You wanted more, Nudelman, and I think Isaac's getting it."

"I think so, too. Listen, will you call everybody tonight? I'd be grateful if you did. I'm pooped."

"OK. Count on me," I said, patting Mandy's head.

"I always do." I was about to get up when he held out his hand to stop me. "Have you got a few more minutes?"

"I'm not buying a truck dealership tonight."

"Very funny, Mendel. Listen, I want to run something by you. There's something I'm struggling with." He looked uncertain, troubled.

"Ask away."

"Mandy's got cancer." The dog looked up as her name was mentioned and gave a single thump of her tail.

"I'm sorry to hear that, Nudelman. I know how attached you are to Mandy." I reached down and scratched Mandy behind the ears to show my sympathy.

"It's a brain tumor. At least that's what Dr. Kessleman thinks."

"That's nasty. I suppose there's nothing to be done."

"That's the question, Mendel. Things can be done. There's a clinic in Pittsburgh with a CAT scan. Don't make a joke. It's a device that surveys the brain so that they can locate the tumor and determine if it's operable."

"Yes, I've read of such things but not for dogs."

"That's what's eating away at me, Mendel. I love this mutt. But the whole bill—diagnosis, operation—would be maybe $3,000."

"You're asking me, should you spend the money? You know what I would say. Mandy is old. Put her away, when the time comes, with a minimum of suffering. Get another dog. Give the money to famine relief for starving children or to World Health to save the millions of children who die of things like diarrhea."

"I could do both."

"So, have you given it?"

"Some, but not that much."

"If you are thinking of doing both, then I say give twice as much to the children and still give Mandy a quiet death.

And while it's on my mind, when the time comes, if you're still around, do the same for me."

"I knew you'd say that, Mendel."

"Then why did you ask me?"

"I suppose I had to hear it from you."

"I guess I better get home if I'm going to make those calls."

Nudelman followed me to the door and gave me a bear hug.

# TWENTY-NINE
# The Sheep Fold

Save me from another Board meeting, and not just any meeting but the one that could put Lev back on a plane to Moscow. They had all been briefed. A summary of the latest misfortunes written by, you guessed it, was in front of each of them. I looked around the table. The mood was reserved; there was none of the usual paraphernalia. Harriet Rosenzweig didn't have a crossword puzzle. Finkelstein didn't have the sports page. Roe didn't have a printout. Sophie Feld didn't have her knitting. Rabbi Bing wasn't jotting down notes for his next sermon.

As for Nudelman, he looked miserable, like a hound that had let the fox slip away. Maybe it was the Youngstown deal. It had fallen through at the last minute. Maybe not. In fact, my little summary was depressing. It didn't just report that Lev had taken the rap for the computer caper. In the few days since the FBI had shown up, the news had gotten even worse. Rosenzweig had received a notice of intended decision. The judge was going to rule that the school was inconsistent with the purpose of the trust. In the spirit of compromise, the school year could play out and the school could even be continued in the building in the future as long as the Board found money from another source to operate it. It could be better; it could be worse. Rosenzweig called it "a dark victory." Nudelman called the judge "Solomon from hell."

On top of this, the Jews for Jesus had decided to move into town. Two guys with hats and curly beards started passing out cartoon pamphlets with New Testament quotes in front of the Monoganessen County Bank, right next to the ATM. This would have gone unnoticed if Morley hadn't decided to interview them. Of course, they acknowledged being there because of the widely circulated claims that Lev was the Messiah. No, he wasn't, they insisted, as the Messiah had already come and gone two thousand years before.

Morley had followed up with a call to Rabbi Bing who was quoted as saying, "At least we can agree on the first point." Not a bad quip for Rabbi Bing, who isn't exactly a Jewish Bill Cosby.

Finally, there was the letter from the Immigration Service asking the Board for its attitude toward the deportation proceedings. I had attached it, as there was no way it could be summarized.

"What does this letter mean?" asked Finkelstein, who apparently agreed with me. "Do they want us to make the decision for them? Isn't it their responsibility, after all? What do they want, a referendum?"

"It's like the probation department giving advice to the judge," said Harriet Rosenzweig, looking over the top of her half-lens reading glasses.

"Will it make any difference?"

"Let's not get hung up on that," said Nudelman. "We've got one question to decide: Do we stick with Lev Kyol for the rest of the semester or not? I would like to hear from each of you, what you honestly feel we should do."

No one said anything although I could feel the words struggling to escape from their throats. Nudelman looked around the table and finally said, "Rabbi Bing, why don't you begin."

The rabbi peered out of his crystalline lenses and ran his hand over his flattened, thinning hair. He was obviously conflicted. The rabbi had two voices—one for everyday use and one for the pulpit—and I wondered which he would be using. It was the everyday one.

"I must confess that I am deeply troubled by the Messiah question."

"You mean there's a question?" asked Finkelstein.

"This week I attended a colloquium in Bloomington, as some of you know. It was on the subject of intermarriage. And every rabbi asked me about Lev, virtually every one of them There were no less than thirty-two."

"What did you tell them?" Harriet Rosenzweig asked.

"I made light of it. I told him that Lev had done nothing himself to propagate the idea. Some of the rabbis remembered my predecessor, and his miraculous curative powers. Needless to say our community appears quite ridiculous at this moment. Some of the comments were rather derisive. They are calling Bolton, Chelm Pennsylvania. I was shaken by the experience."

Everyone looked at him, expecting more. "There was a professor from the seminary, Pinsky, noted for his original ideas. Pinsky whispered to me, quite confidentially, at a reception... You know, when the talk is...well, never mind."

"What did he say?" asked Finkelstein with impatience.

Rabbi Bing shook his head and chuckled to himself. "Only that the Messiah was overdue and that we shouldn't be so negative. That we had no faith, no spirit, that the Holocaust was a genocide of more than people. It was a killer of our collective belief. That we are functioning as spiritual zombies, going through the ossified motions, words to that effect." Rabbi Bing's pale cheeks began to bloom with embarrassment. "You have to understand that Pinsky is a Jewish mystic of sorts."

"Whether or not we think he's the Messiah is less important than what the Pentecostals think," said Harriet.

"They shouldn't be greedy. They've already had theirs; it's our turn," quipped Finkelstein. I laughed, and so did Nudelman.

What followed was a little like a movie I saw about a jury deciding a murder case. Everything went into the soup kettle. Rabbi Bing, for example, was trying hard to be impartial but his resentment of the school as a rival Jewish institution shown like wood through a bad paint job. If only Lev hadn't accepted the blame for the computer theft, for the Rabbi just couldn't see how we could keep a director who had admitted to criminal conduct.

Sophie Feld thought the dinner was in bad taste, but she was a renowned cook and was bound to give the matter a gastronomic slant. Beyond that she approved of the purpose and was glad we were helping the homeless.

Sharp as always, Harriet Rosenzweig argued that there was more to be lost than gained in terminating Lev with no more than a month left in the year. Besides the future of the school was in doubt. Where would we get the money to run it next year? As for the Messiah business, it would pass.

Finkelstein talked about the Palestinian and the Messiah controversies and said that with only a month to go we could just as well get rid of him now.

Of course, Roe went on and on about the rape of his computer and the embarrassment it had caused him at the insurance company. There were even suspicions that he had been a part of it, what with his position on the Board, and that his daughter Suzy had been implicated. Poor Roe.

What surprised me about the discussion was the lack of animosity. Oh, there was passion enough and intensity, but each of them seemed to accept that, even with all the turbulence and trouble, a lot of good had come out of the school and Lev's erratic leadership.

Nudelman summed it up. "Who would have imagined that when we started the school we would find ourselves in such a goldfish bowl? But I have to say that knowing what I now know, I would do it over again. Why? Because it's given Isaac something he would never have gotten from the school district. It's hard for me to say just what, but if I could put it in one word I would say sympathy, or maybe it's compassion. And I think it's because of the school and Lev's leadership." He looked around for confirmation but all he got was another round of monologue.

All this time, I sat there on the first car of a rollercoaster ever climbing and waiting for the sickening descent. So far no one had asked for my opinion. As I wasn't a Board member I had no intention of volunteering one. I remained torn between wanting him out of town and wanting him to stay on as director.

After two hours without putting the question to a vote, Rabbi Bing looked at me and invited my opinion.

"He's a good person, an original thinker, a good leader. Not the most practical person I've met. But I agree with Nudelman. We've got so little time to go, why rock the boat."

"Rock the boat?" shouted Finkelstein. "The boat is on its way to the bottom."

"You asked, so that's my opinion. Stand behind him."

"Anything else?" asked Nudelman. "Secret ballot. Yes, we keep him. No, we terminate him."

I passed out little pieces of notepaper and got seven back. There was silence as I unfolded each. I must say my heart was on fast time as I recorded the votes: yes, yes, no, no, no, no. Yes. He was out.

Nudelman took it with a sigh and a shrug. "This is a mistake," he said. And when they had all left with the somber tone of a funeral party, he said to me. "You tell him, Mendel."

"Why me? It wasn't my doing."

"That's why."

# THIRTY

# At Supper

They were eating when I came, all of them eating together in the dining room: the teachers at a long table with Lev at the center, the old folks at their table, the homeless at theirs and the students at the rest. Lev saw me and invited me to join them. The room was echoing with children's voices, the clatter of utensils on metal and dishes, the scrape of chairs, and the air was flavored with celery and carrot soup.

Lev looked peaked but in a better mood than the last time. The rest of the faculty seemed weary except for Harney, who was at the moment fondling a piece of lettuce. A morose Schweig was on the end, keeping his own counsel.

"As you see, Mendel, we celebrate first fruit of little garden." I sat down across from him, choked with my bad news. "Mr. Harney, our guests, and children are expanding garden already. We now have also three milk cows and laying hens. Not only will we feed everyone we may even sell some to make money."

"The children do their turn as well?"

"Most are loving it. As for homeless, it gives a future. Simple work, of course, but there is always need for help on farm."

The more he talked about the school, the future, the more I began to feel like someone had draped a wet towel over my face. My anxiety was making it hard for me to breathe. I got up and told him I needed some air and asked him to meet me by the bench in front of the building.

I rushed out of the dining hall and the building and walked the grounds in the heavy evening air. A small hand-push cultivator was parked on the edge of a large field beyond the existing raised beds, the dark freshly turned earth giving off a pungent smell. The sound of a car with a hole in its muffler jarred me and I waited as it passed and faded out of sight, between the rolling hills. I walked to the barn and saw the three cows, black and white, tethered in clean stalls. One gave me a vacant stare with its dark defenseless eyes and I saw, in its place, innocent Lev. I left the barn and walked back to the front of the building past a newly planted flower garden. Coming around the corner of the building I saw Lev, bending over a rose.

"Feel like a little walk?" I asked. He nodded, and we ambled down the winding gravel drive between the elms that had somehow survived a recent plague. We walked along the gravel berm of the county road, beside a rusted barbed-wire fence and a rolling green pasture, where several cows grazed. He spoke of complex forms to be completed for certification of the school and some new textbooks that he and the faculty were reviewing.

"Who has been helping you on the teaching staff?" I asked. "Someone who could do what you are doing if you were sick?"

He looked down and kicked a stone. "Why?"

I had to tell him outright. "When you took the blame for the computer theft, the Board had another meeting." I couldn't bring myself to say it.

"And?"

"They decided they couldn't keep you on." The words caught in my throat. "If only you hadn't said that, it might have been different. It was very close."

"It's not law question, Mendel. Responsibility is moral question." His voice was steady but I could see that his eyes were teary. "As director I must take responsibility for what happens." We walked on, the scraping of gravel the only sound between us. He looked at me, his long face sad and grave. "So they will send me back?"

"I don't know, Lev. That's up to the immigration authority."

"I see. In that case, you must ask Shusterman to take over when the time comes."

"I'm sorry."

"Don't be. I have done what I set out to do." There was restrained sadness but no bitterness in his tone.

"But this is only the beginning."

"Moses didn't get to the Promised Land," he said. "Is there anything I must do? Must I leave?"

"No, you can stay in your apartment through the end of the semester at least. Just make an announcement, however you want, tomorrow. And give up your duties to another."

"When?"

"Immediately, I'm afraid."

"As soon as that." There was disbelief in his voice.

A truck passed, and we crowded away from the pavement.

It was over just like that. I felt as though I'd just set down a heavy bag of groceries. He had made it so easy. No recriminations, no chest beating. I might have told him that the store was out of his favorite cereal.

As we walked back he talked about the garden. One of the homeless men had already been offered a job at a nearby dairy and Lev intended to find another homeless person to take his place. He wanted the school to be a permanent way station for the needy, wanted the children to understand them and help them. He left me at my car with a handshake and an expression that showed no hint of animosity.

"Goodbye, my friend," was all he said.

On the way home I thought about his restraint. He felt deeply for the school and wanted to remain. It came to me that he had held back as much as he could just to spare me. It was as if, having lost his job because he accepted the blame for the computer theft, he was willing to relieve me, and even the Board, of the pain of having to tell him. Even so, I felt guilt, for my silence in his office and for my hoping he would leave.

# THIRTY-ONE

# Reprieve

E stelle was to come home that night. I must have called six times before she finally answered. For some reason I wanted to be the first to tell her, as if I could somehow sculpt the words into some shape that would hurt her less.

She sounded weary on the phone but agreed to let me come over and have tea. No, she hadn't talked to anyone yet. She hadn't even unpacked. Yes, her sister was fine and even sent her regards, but the weather had been rotten.

She met me at the door in her floral bathrobe, a good sign that we were still close. Her hair was tied in a towel turban. She smelled of carnation soap and her eyes looked lost, without the usual highlights, but no less curious.

We went to the kitchen and sat down at the maple table our cups surrounded by a pile of unopened mail.

"I get so many solicitations, and would you believe it? Even though Sam's been dead eight years the Veterans of Foreign Wars still sends him the annual dues notice and magazine." She picked it up to show me. "It's positively creepy."

"Somebody said old soldiers never die."

"General MacArthur."

She opened an envelope, glanced at the contents, put it down and finally met my eyes for a moment with a quick shot of familiarity that gave me a lift.

"What's been happening here in Bolton?"

"I thought you should know that they've given Lev the ax." Each word weighed fifty pounds.

Estelle looked like she'd gotten an electric shock as she said, "No. They just couldn't. Not now."

"Well, they did. He took all the blame for the computer business and it was the last of the hay."

"The last straw."

"Yes, straw."

"What about Nudelman?"

"He was against it. And so was I."

She was biting her lip and thinking so hard I could feel the brain waves. "Will they deport him for this?"

"Could be. He's confessed to a crime, not to mention the little red lie on the application about his job."

She muttered something to herself.

"What?"

"I'll have to marry him. It'll be the only way to keep him here." My heart stopped. "But you were thinking about that anyway?"

"Mendel, you don't understand anything."

"I understand you and he have been pretty close."

She dismissed this with a wave of her hand.

For once anger made me boil. I could feel it in my face as I said, "What in hell's going on inside your head? As maybe your closest friend I deserve to know. Enough mystery! Enough already!" I felt better already.

"There's no point in keeping it from you now; now that he's out."

"Keep what?"

She stared at me looking unsure what to do.

"It's not what you think at all. I had no intention of marrying Lev. True, I like him and he's a good friend."

"So?"

"I know something about him that, had the Board found it out, they might have relieved him earlier."

"What?"

"He has cancer. A brain tumor."

My heart sunk in my chest. It all came together: all the symptoms, the headaches, the fall, his passivity, his willingness to take risks. He had the integrity of someone who could suffer nothing worse than what was already happening to him.

"Can't something be done?"

"It's inoperable. That's why I've been taking him to Pittsburgh. He even had one of those cat scans. He'll be paralyzed in a few months. That and more." She was tearful, stricken.

That explained it all. I was shocked but relieved in a way and guilty because of it. I had never before acknowledged relief at the death of another, except for Hitler and a few of his cohorts. But there it was, and I was ashamed.

"So now you have the secret." Her lips drew together as if she were afraid to say any more.

"Shouldn't he at least get some treatment? What is it, chemotherapy, something?"

"He won't have it. He says he didn't come here to be a parasite on our medical system, especially when he sees so many people who aren't getting any help at all, people who have lived here all their lives." Estelle picked up another envelope, one from the Cancer Society. "I guess I should give some more to this one."

"When did this come up?"

"He knew when he left Russia that the tumor was inoperable."

"Then why did he come? Was it to get treatment?"

"No. I asked him that. He told me that he wanted to do something in his life, make a memory. He felt his life had been meaningless so far."

"My God."

"You see, Mendel. It was never what you thought."

She looked at me with earnest expectation and I assumed she was waiting for me to complete the conversation we'd begun after I saw them both in Pittsburgh. But I couldn't. It was as if I only had the will to go beyond our coffee klatch when I thought it was impossible. Now that she was again within my reach I backed off. What was wrong with me! One of those moments of awful indecision struck me like a fit of shaking. I felt myself to be in a bubble unable to break out. I opened my mouth, but nothing came. A voice inside told me that I was a fool. I agreed.

The bubble broke and I forced myself, like a chronic stutterer, to say, "I'm relieved, Estelle."

She took my hand and it felt like static running up my arm. "Then we must talk about it again." Her face changed, became full of strange deep light, or so it seemed to me.

"About what?" I found myself saying, and if it were physically possible I would have kicked myself in the behind. "Sorry, of course we must, and will, but given what you've just told me about him, I couldn't begin to muster the words."

"Now you know what I've been carrying around like a heavy suitcase."

"You could have told me."

"How? You're the Board liaison. You'd have been bound to spill it to Nudelman."

"You're sure he can't be convinced to take some treatment."

"Don't you think I've tried?" Her eyes glossed over with frustration and anguish. "You don't know what it took just to drag him to the specialist in Pittsburgh."

"I'm going to tell Nudelman." I got up, resolved to start at once to get him reinstated.

"Why? Hasn't Lev got enough trouble?"

"I'm going to try to get the Board to cancel their decision, if for no other reason than to give him a decent death. I think it can be done. After all, a brain tumor. Everything he did was because of that. The vote was close." My mind filled with the things I could say to persuade them.

"Give it a try, Mendel." She put both of her hands on my shoulders and looked into my eyes with approval. "At least you'll feel better having tried."

"Does anybody else know?"

"Not a soul."

"Can I go to him and talk about it?"

"Absolutely not. No. Just do the best you can for him."

She gave me a kiss on the cheek, as light as what my little childhood girlfriend used to call butterfly-wings, and she dismissed me with a gentle shove. I left her, still feeling it on my cheek.

I called Nudelman from my apartment and for the first time in weeks he didn't sound like a voice from another world.

"You sound good, Nudelman," I said putting some butter on him before I hit him with the news.

"I do feel good." The Youngstown deal is back on. The bankruptcy trustee supports it."

"I'm happy for you. Soon every truck in western Pennsylvania will be from Quality Trucks."

"Mendel, be glad you're not a businessman. You're always looking to get bigger, increase your sales, your profit, your yield on equity. It's nerve-wracking."

"But you wouldn't change places."

"Have you ever met somebody who would? So, what's on your mind?"

I told him, and he was stunned. I could hear the heavy breathing. "We've got to get the Board to reverse field," he said. "The tumor made him do the crazy things he did."

"They weren't so crazy, Nudelman. Just courageous and moral."

"For the average person, that combination is crazy. I'm sorry to tell you." Maybe he was right. "Mendel, thanks for all the help during this trying period, but I'll take care of the Board myself. I've been wrong to dump it on you. You're a pushover for doing other people's laundry, Mendel."

That same night I got a call from Nudelman. He had already done it—on the phone, yet. Every member of the Board had voted to restore Lev to his position, but on condition that the tumor was the real thing, not just some story hammered together to save his job.

"After all," Nudelman explained, "he's told some fibs before."

"But this came from Estelle!"

"She's in cahoots with him, everybody knows that. She even does his laundry. Don't take it personally, Mendel. And one thing more. Since you had to give him the bad news, we want you to tell him the good news, although nothing could be good news to somebody in his shoes..." Nudelman's voice petered out.

"I'll do it, with Estelle's help."

"Good idea."

I went to sleep that night satisfied that I had made up for part of my bad feelings toward him. But in the end, it was just bogus bills that I had paid him with.

# THIRTY-TWO

# Overcoming the World

O range juice, with its tart sweet chill, was flowing down my throat when the phone rang, and I choked and coughed on it as I answered. It was Selma and she sounded as if the school had burned down.

"I didn't know who to call, but somehow I knew it should be you, Mendel."

"What's happened?"

"It's Lev," she said, her voice shattering. "I don't want to talk about it. Just come as soon as you can. I'm in Lev's office with Maimonides."

I turned off the coffee, swilled another glass of juice, and was on my way like a firefighter down the greased pole. And that's not far from fact. I drove like a policeman and even skidded my tires on the gravel of the school parking lot, wondering all the while what I would find, but dreading to think that he was already dead; a sudden collapse of his system. I rushed up the hall, banging my thigh on the corner of a table, and barged into the office unprepared for what I saw.

Mi and Selma were seated next to each other at the desk as if they were being interviewed by Lev. Lev was in his chair, sprawled back, his head tilted to one side, his arms wide and drooping toward the floor. I stared and felt the strength flow out of my legs.

Maimonides and Selma were wearing that black cast of helplessness, shock, and fear that mask the living on first sight of the dead. I shared it too. I was both heavy and numb, as if my heart had been shot with Novocain.

"I found him like that," said Selma. "I brought him some tea and toast this morning. I sometimes do that. Otherwise he would forget to eat." She gazed at the toast. "He must have been here all night this way."

"That's why we called you first, Mendel," said Maimonides, pushing his multi-colored *keepah* a little higher on the grey remnants of his hair. "Given his resemblance to, well, Christ on the cross, sprawled out that way, and considering the attention he has received from unorthodox Christian sources—".

"He left a note," said Selma.

I reached for it. It was written on school stationary in his Cyrillic-looking script that I found hard to read. But this was very clear, as if he wanted to be understood.

"I know this is not right," he had written. "As Jews we are told to go on living and hoping until we die. But it would be selfish for me to do so. My body must die soon. I have done what I could in my short time, done it with love for the stranger and the friend alike. Make of my life what you will. Some of you may take comfort from it. Lev Kyol."

I let the note drop on the desk and my arm fell limp. He had taken his own life rather than face paralysis and the loss of memory and reason. My eyes fogged over with sorrow, regret, and yes, guilt. I recovered enough to look around his desk for the pills; it couldn't have been anything else. There it was, next to an empty glass: an empty pill bottle with a prescription from Dr. Zucker—sleeping pills.

"Why did he do this, Mendel? Was it because the Board dismissed him?"

"No, Selma. He was ill. Incurably ill."

"But he never let us know." She sounded almost angry that he had deprived her of a chance to help and console him. She began to weep quietly, put her hands over her face and turned away.

"It's so strange," said Maimonides. "We haven't had a death here for so long. And he was so young, so much younger than we all are." His gnarled, white fingers with their loose flesh began to twitch and he clasped them together.

"We've got to call Dr. Zucker," I said.

"Should we move him? We can't let people find him like that. If it got out, the *meshugena* would be sure he's Jesus come back a second time," said Mi, casting a foreboding glance at Lev's cruciform body.

Maimonides was right; anyone who saw Lev would imagine a cross behind him. "Selma, call Dr. Zucker. Mi and I will try to put his arms on his chest or something."

I was just going around the desk when Bron and one of the homeless walked in through the half-open door.

"Lev, one of the cows is sick. Wally, here, found her lying on her side in her stall. We wanted... Excuse me, I didn't know there was a meeting. " Bron lifted his hand to his head. "Is he?"

"Yes."

The other man was standing half-behind Bron. He looked like he'd just seen a paraplegic get up out of a wheelchair.

"Do you see the way he is? They are right about him." He looked at each of us for confirmation, and seeing none, he turned around and rushed out the door.

Maimonides looked at me. "What should we do?"

"Don't disturb him," I said, immediately thinking myself a fool. "It's too late. Besides, it would be disrespectful."

"Why?"

"His last wish. Let people make of him whatever they want to."

"But Mendel, there'll be a real *balagan*."

"Probably," I said, starting to feel good about my decision. "Why should it be any different after he's dead? He wanted to be remembered."

I could already hear the echo of many footsteps in the hall.

# THIRTY-THREE

# Credo

W ho took the picture, the one that made the front page the next day? I'm not sure. Considering the poor quality, it must have been a cheap little flea market camera. Morley wouldn't say where he got it, only that he had paid someone a hundred dollars for the film. It wasn't me and it couldn't have been Selma or Maimonides. It must have been one of the homeless who crowded into the room with the ferocious intensity and curiosity that people have for human tragedy, at least when they are no more than witnesses.

We let them look, what could we do. Not everybody thought they had seen something holy. There was at least one scoffer, and one man even accused the school of faking it just to get some more national attention and possible contributions.

We finally managed to get them out and lock the door until Dr. Zucker and the funeral home van could come. Selma and I sat quietly, sadly, listening to the milling buzz of the crowd of children and faculty that had gathered outside the door.

Dr. Zucker didn't take more than half an hour to get there. He was a slight man with close-set blue eyes and a mushy way of speaking. If he felt anything as he gave Lev his last medical examination, he didn't show it. He was calm and matter of fact. A doctor gets used to death.

When we mentioned the position of Lev's arms, he just shrugged and said, "People don't choose where or how. I've seen people in the bathroom; heard of, but never seen, one in the act of making love; people doing things they wouldn't want others to see. I'm afraid this is commonplace. Poor Lev just slumped back in his chair and his arms flopped down." As he said this he was already moving them.

He picked up the empty bottle of pills and looked at the label. "I prescribed these just a few days ago. He'd been having trouble sleeping, so he said. He must have downed the whole bottle. About thirty too many. There'll be an autopsy, I'm afraid. And the Burial Society won't take him. They won't accept suicides in the cemetery, you know, Mendel. Too bad. Not having any relatives here."

I took the bottle and threw it into the wastebasket. To be sure it wouldn't be discovered I reached down and covered it with scrap paper. Dr. Zucker looked at me as if I'd pulled a gun on him.

"I'm sorry, that won't do, Mendel. I've got to certify the cause of death. Certify."

"Did you know he had an incurable brain tumor?"

"Why, no. He never told me. How do you know?" I could see he didn't believe me.

"Estelle told me. She took him to see a specialist in Pittsburgh."

"Estelle." He was beginning to accept it. Dr. Zucker didn't want to see Lev buried in the potter's field either.

"I'm sure that's what killed him," I said.

"So am I," said Selma, who had been silently cheering me on.

He hesitated. I looked out the window and saw the county sheriff's tan patrol car pulling up the drive.

"Estelle can put you in touch with the doctor. He had maybe a month to live."

"I think that will suffice for the death certificate," said Dr. Zucker with obvious reluctance.

"Good." At least he could be buried among us. I've done something for him. I looked at Selma and we exchanged smiles of understanding.

By the time Morley Rasmussen got there, Dr. Zucker was just snapping his leather tool kit shut and the deputy sheriff, Doris Rutkowski, was trying to stuff her notebook into her back pocket. It was at least two hours before poor Lev was taken to the O'Connor Funeral Home.

I waited until the O'Connor van had left before making my calls to Estelle and Nudelman.

"The poor, dear man. I'll miss him. But maybe it was better this way," she said in an uneven, tearful way.

"We'll all miss him."

Next, I called Nudelman and gave him the details. I could hear the gears of his mind grinding. A quick and quiet funeral was his solution.

"Thanks again, Mendel, for all you've done. I'll handle the rest." I was about to hang up when he said, "Mendel?"

"Yes."

"We put Mandy to sleep today. No heroic measures."

"I'm sorry, Nudelman."

"It was very hard. But I want you to know I'm giving $1,500 to CARE."

"Make it in Lev's memory."

Before leaving the office, I poked around, looking at the objects and projects left behind by Lev. A yellowed snapshot of his sister in a park, an open file with school certification applications, the minutes of the curriculum committee, a pencil dented with tooth marks, a few loose hairs, the brass samovar given to him by Miriam Edelstein—now cold and out of place. I felt like a hollow tree.

Morley did it again. He was Lev's Paul, except that unlike the disciples, he had no aura of belief. He was just reporting the facts as he saw them. And the facts were that a man, believed by some to be Christ returned to earth, had died once again on the cross in the form of an old swivel chair. The picture, taken without the benefit of a flash, was pretty dark and, I thought, morbid.

Even before the story broke on the evening news, someone had already stolen a lot of Lev's clothes from his apartment. Sad. What could anyone get out of an old pair of Soviet undershorts, even if they had been worn by a good, maybe holy, man? Wouldn't remembrance of the deeds be better?

The next day Doris, the deputy sheriff, had to be called to control the crowds flocking to the school just to have a look around. Some made off with souvenirs, if you could call that fine lettuce they were raising in the garden a souvenir. Hopefully the thieves put it in a salad and were the better for it.

I spoke with Nudelman and Estelle many times over the next day or so before the funeral. Nudelman made sure that Dr. Zucker didn't have second thoughts about the cause of death, so that Lev could be buried in the cemetery. The Board took up a collection, bought a plot and paid for the funeral arrangements. Most of them were feeling guilty for having sacked Lev, even though they hadn't been told of his sickness.

Nudelman seemed to be making up for having left so much to me. He handled everything. The funeral was to be held at the school so that the children and the teachers could be there. The burial would be smaller, with just a few of us attending.

Estelle and the sisterhood planned to provide the food for people who were likely to attend—the Board, the faculty, the children, the homeless and no doubt a few of the community church people. In addition to Rabbi Bing, one of the children and a member of the faculty were to speak. All of this came to me by phone.

Nudelman searched the papers for any sign that the Messiah story had been repeated but there was no sign that it had. No one wanted the funeral to turn into a spectacle.

# THIRTY-FOUR

# By Man Came Also

I had my black pants on and was rummaging in my closet for my most conservative tie when Nudelman called.

"Mendel, I need your advice."

"What's up?" I asked. "You want me to do something at the funeral?"

"No, I'm afraid there isn't going to be a funeral. Not today at least."

"Don't tell me Dr. Zucker changed his mind?"

"No. Mr. O'Connor just called to tell me that Lev's body is missing." I felt a rushing in my ears. On top of everything. "They had him all prepared the night before. Just a few final touches to be put on before they got him dressed and laid him out. This morning, when one of the assistants looked in the drawer in their refrigerated room, he wasn't there. Maybe someone put him in the wrong drawer, they thought, so they looked in every drawer. Then they double-checked the two other people who were laid out in two of the parlors. No, they hadn't made that kind of mistake, although Mr. O'Connor said it had happened once before."

"What did they do, call the police?"

"You're getting ahead of me. First, they contacted the night attendant. The man doesn't have lab experience, but he receives unexpected visitors and brings coffee to the people who keep an all- night vigil. As far as he knew no one had come and gotten the body. True, he had left the building for an hour to have a burger and a beer at Andy's All-Night Grill at about 3:00 a.m. The front door had been open as always, but the door to the prep room and lab was locked, or so he thought. They did find a side window open a crack. So what do you think?"

"What do I think? You mean theologically?"

"No, the funeral. We have to cancel it don't we?"

"How can you have a funeral without the dead person?"

"Of course. You know, Mendel, I'm a hard guy to rattle but this is getting to me."

We called the school and told them to put up a sign: Funeral Postponed. I told Estelle and the ladies to freeze the cakes and the chopped liver and the other things. Those who could be notified, were, but we didn't tell anyone why. In the meantime, the police put out an all-points bulletin for a missing body, complete with description.

I finally changed out of my black pants and went to see Estelle. She greeted me at the door with a roll of freezer wrap and a scowl.

"What's going on? You don't just cancel a funeral on short notice. It's not the same as a…a baseball game after all, especially this one."

"Estelle, what do you need to have a funeral? Take a guess. More than anything?"

"A coffin?"

"More than that—a dead person!"

"You mean he's not dead?" She dropped the freezer wrap.

"I mean he's missing."

Her face crumpled into incredulous disgust. "Some crazies must have stolen him. It's the messiah *meshugena*."

"So maybe it's true," I said.

"Mendel, you don't mean that."

"Maybe he went to heaven."

"Be serious."

"Be serious. How can I be serious with these kinds of goings-on?"

"The phone," she said and went to answer it. "It's for you."

"Who is it, the Pope?"

"It's Morley."

"Tell him I'm out of town."

"He says he knows all about Lev and can't find Rabbi Bing and he wants a quote from somebody in the Jewish community before he puts the story on the wire."

I went to the phone. Feeling like a mafioso called to a grand jury I answered, "No comment. We don't know any more than you do, Morley, maybe even less." That was that.

And that was how I was quoted. Sort of. By the time Morley got done reshaping my words, I seemed to be acknowledging something supernatural. Fortunately, mine wasn't the only quote in the article. There was a Jesuit professor of theology who discussed the religious basis of the second coming theory, a Baptist minister who doubted it had happened, a police detective who thought it was the work of organ thieves, and a famous televangelist who claimed to have seen a silvery vision soaring up to the heavens at precisely 3:17 a.m. Eastern Standard Time. He knew the time because his digital clock had stopped at the very moment and he had just gotten a new battery. Once again, Bolton was in the national news. By now, Morley must have been dreaming of a Pulitzer Prize.

This went on for a week while the police did an identification check on every derelict person found dead in vacant lots, doorways, alleys, culverts and under bridge abutments. Not one fit the description. There were reports by people who claimed they saw Lev in different parts of the country: sitting in a bus terminal in Hannibal, Missouri; on a ferry boat in Seattle; praying alone in a Catholic church in New Haven; preaching to tourists waiting in line for a cable car in San Francisco.

The police tracked down Elmo Riegle in Texarkana, Texas, where he was saving souls. It was not his doing. He was 1,500 miles away from Bolton. They followed other leads—a couple of known Satanists from Squirrel Hill, and a witch's coven in Sewickley—but nothing came of any of it. They gave up. There were, after all, a few more pressing matters, what with drugs, child abuse, and all. Case closed.

Another Board meeting—this one to decide whether to have a posthumous funeral—and the question was hotly debated. In the end, it was decided that a funeral was more to honor the memory of a person. There was no need for a body. It was the spirit that mattered.

"Besides," said Finkelstein, "we can't get a refund on the casket and the chopped liver won't keep forever, not to mention the tea cakes."

Rabbi Bing thought his humor in bad taste but there was more than one stifled chuckle. I was sure Lev would have laughed.

## THIRTY-FIVE

# Hallelujah

After a two-week delay everyone thought that there would be a nice quiet ceremony. After all, the news of Lev's disappearance hadn't occupied the media for more than a few days. Initially the Board had decided just to have a memorial service and to dispense with the burial altogether, since there was nothing to bury. Besides, it would be better not to waste a grave.

But then, two days before the funeral, Sarah Leventhal died in her sleep. Since her broken hip she had been confined to her bed. She was nearly 100, the oldest living schoolteacher in the county, and the first to die among the old folks in nearly 10 years.

I went out to the school immediately, to pay a condolence call and see what I could do to help. All the old folks were sitting at a single long table in the dining room looking frail and vulnerable in that cavernous room. When I got closer, I saw that they were calm and accepting.

As Selma put it, "She had such a long, helping life."

They were speaking about her as if she had just moved to another town. There were even a few laughs at her forgetfulness, which had been increasing of late.

"Tell you what we want to do, Mendel," said Maimonides. "Now don't laugh or think this odd."

"I promise."

"We think we should put Miss Leventhal in that coffin they bought for Lev, and bury her in that grave. She never bought one of her own; she didn't believe in it. One time she told me that buying a cemetery plot is the same as buying a ticket to go someplace you don't want to go."

"We all agree, Mendel. It's just what Lev would have wanted," added Selma.

"Just like killing two birds with one stone," said Izzy Bortz.

It sounded right to me. Nudelman thought about it for a minute and agreed. So did Rabbi Bing. Even Mr. O'Connor went along and threw in free embalming and transportation. He must have been relieved that no one put him on the carpet for losing a body. In fact, rumor has it that he's been asked to speak on mortuary security at the next meeting of the National Funeral Directors Association.

The morning of the funeral, I drove to Estelle's house to help her carry the food. It was a glorious late spring day; the sunlight tinted everything it touched and the air was unusually dry. Estelle was wearing a blue and white silk dress with a floral pattern.

"It was just too nice a day to be somber. Lev would have liked this and Miss Leventhal loved flowers. Remember, she always had a small vase of flowers on her desk, daffodils in the spring and roses in the fall."

We drove out to the school through pools of shade and dappled sunlight. The road wound and rolled over a gentle landscape that had changed very little since I had come to Bolton as a teenager.

We thought we were going to be early but there were at least 200 people gathered in conversational groups or seated on folding chairs on the lawn. It looked more like a graduation than a funeral but what would be expected for two such people. One had been born in the county nearly a century ago and out-lived all of her family. The other had been here for less than a year. Yet each of them had left a permanent mark on the town.

I left Estelle to lay out the food and went up to Nudelman, Finkelstein and Rabbi Bing, who were in some sort of huddle. Rabbi Bing looked preoccupied; Nudelman amused.

"What's up?"

"Well, as you can see, Mendel, we have a large and diverse group of people," said Rabbi Bing.

"A Muslim clergyman from Pittsburgh, a friend of Mumzer Arakat, wants to say a prayer," said Nudelman.

"That's wonderful," I said and meant it.

"And a choir from the AME church wants to sing.

"Fantastic."

In fact, the religious leaders of every denomination in the town said something. Of course Rabbi Bing led off and he was possessed by some emotion that I had never before seen in him. He is a bookish man, shy and dry. But this day, whether it was the presence of all those other men and women of God or the spirit of Lev, he expressed a simple message of human caring with passion.

The Muslim followed, wearing a three-piece suit; he might have been a stockbroker. Rabbi Bing waited as he climbed the two steps of the platform. The rabbi extended his hand and the Muslim took it. He prayed for the end of misunderstanding and hatred between Palestinian and Israeli, and when he had finished he went over to Rabbi Bing, embraced him and said, "My brother." Everyone heard him. Rabbi Bing was startled but he yielded to it.

The unexpected contact, a reflection of the hanging together of the two flags, caused a current of feeling in the crowd. Every minister in the town spoke at least a few words, noting Lev's courage, kindness, and humanity.

Even Mayor Jeff Willis spoke, eulogizing Miss Leventhal. She had been his English teacher. He told of the many Boltonites who had written to her over the years telling her how she had opened the door to literature and poetry for them.

The speeches and prayers over, the chorus of the AME church filed up, wearing shiny red satin robes with gold collars. They were sixty in all and their blended voices resounded against the stone wall of the school with parts of Handel's *Messiah*. They began with "*Glory to God*," repeated with many variations and a prolonged "*and peace on earth*." Next was a more somber and reverent "*Behold the lamb of God that taketh away the sins of the world*." A jubilant "*He is the King of Glory*" followed.

Words are poor tools to describe music so joyous and transcendent. To one without hearing it would be like seeing a great flight of birds wheeling dark against a pure blue sky; the unity, motion, evanescence, and power of a waterfall; the diminishing intensity of a failing sun that leaves behind a stain of brilliant orange-red afterglow.

As I listened it came to me that the music itself was a lesson. The harmonies and rhythms made a sound greater than each voice, greater in an immeasurable way than the parts. A human had written it but the music only had life when others played and sang it. More than the words and the melodies, it said that no living thing could exist alone. All of life, from the lowest protein to the human, was dependent. And it was a testament of our potential, of what one person with the help of others, could accomplish. This was the eulogy of Lev, of Miss Leventhal, and also a tribute to Nudelman—a celebration of the possible. They finished with the "Hallelujah Chorus," but done in the complex tempos and harmonies of an Afro-American spiritual, and the audience clapped with them to the beat.

It seemed that for those two hours, hatred, misunderstanding, envy, indifference didn't exist, and a community of shared values united us. That can happen with a crowd. We saw it, felt it at the dinner for the homeless, felt it again at the celebration of the stateless, and we felt it that fair spring day.

Rabbi Bing gave a benediction and six of us—Maimonides and me, Bron and Cohan, Isaac Nudelman and Sami Arakat—carried the coffin to the hearse for the last ride. What were we carrying as the choir sang *kyrie eleison* following behind us? Not Lev, not even Miss Leventhal. What was inside the grey metal box, I imagined, was as powerful as what my ancestors carried in the Ark of the Covenant. We carried hope—hope and the understanding that we were all capable of so much more.

# THIRTY-SIX

# Life Insurance

If the disappearance of Lev's body wasn't enough, something else happened that couldn't easily be explained. The staff of the school had some fringe benefits to compensate for their poor salaries. A group life insurance policy provided the beneficiaries with $10,000. There was a clause that excluded suicide as a cause of death, but Dr. Zucker's death certificate had taken care of that. When we looked at Lev's employment records we found that he had not bothered to name a beneficiary. As you might expect I was asked to find one. Surely someone, even a cousin, must be around who would consider $10,000 the equivalent of winning the Irish Sweepstakes. My first thought was that the Russian consulate in New York City would help. They agreed to track Lev down if I could provide enough information about his identity. I faxed everything Nudelman had and sent it to a Mr. Korshakov, tracer of lost citizens.

Weeks passed. Nothing. I called. A couple of days later he responded. "Be patient. Soviet Union big country. Sun rises, sun sets, same time." I accepted his advice. Until one day, after

I had given up hope of ever hearing from him, an official letter arrived from the consulate, fortunately written in English.
"Official records show that Lev Abramovich Kyol, a pedagogue, died in the siege of Leningrad in 1944 of pneumonia." I
read it over three times wondering what to do with it. It wasn't
my responsibility, I finally decided. I went to see Nudelman,
and found him in the driveway, washing his car. He saw me,
greeted me with a big smile and turned back to wiping the
bubbles of water off the hood. He stood back, wrung out the
rag and admired his work.

"Washing a car, shaving, spraying the roses, are the kind
of tasks that give you a quick shot of satisfaction, don't you
agree, Mendel?"

"To tell the truth, I never thought much about it," I
answered. Getting right to the point, I handed him the letter. He
gave it back, rubbed his hands dry on his jeans, and took it again.

He looked up at me, his eyes squinting skeptically, and
said, "Impossible. They've just screwed up."

"You're probably right, Nudelman. What would you expect
from Soviet bureaucrats. What do we do?"

Nudelman looked at the hood, rubbed a stain off with his
thumb and looked back. "Tell the insurance company that we
couldn't locate any survivors."

I looked at him. "You're sure?"

"Mendel, we've had enough controversy already. Enough's
enough."

And so, I put the letter in Lev's personnel file and that
was that.

But it wasn't. Newspaper reports on the death and now
disappearance of his body recurred. An NBC television news

crew came to town to do a feature on Lev for national syndication. They ran around taking pictures of the grave, the old folks home, and interviewed a few people at random. Nudelman, (not me), and the Rabbi, were filmed, asking "Was it possible that Lev Kyol was the second coming of Jesus?"

The program aired a month later. I watched it. There was Nudelman watering his lawn. And his answer to the big question was "Anything is possible." At least that's the only part of the interview they put on the screen. TV, it seems, never has enough time. They talked with someone, a woman in Slippery Rock, who swore that she had seen a ghostly figure soaring across the moon the night Lev's body disappeared, but it could have been an airplane. Rabbi Bing told them that Lev was a good person, but the Jewish people are still waiting for the Messiah, and not holding their collective breath. The longest interview—about three minutes—was a theologian from a bible college in South Carolina. His answer to the big question was "maybe." The interviewer, a captivating blond with a lilting Southern accent, pushed him a little. She reviewed the evidence: the way Lev had reached out to the poor and brought different groups together; she raised some analogies to the Gospel; and finished off with the missing body and questionable identity.

The theologian answered, "The people who believe that this man was Lord Jesus come back again to set an example for the rest of us, they don't need what the lawyers might call a preponderance of the evidence to prove the point. They accept it on faith. What most people don't understand is that like, say, quantum mechanics, if you know what that is, faith has its own rules."

"What rules?" she asked.

"Well, the most important rule of faith is that the acceptance of something as true isn't founded on the weight of evidence." His voice took on a Sunday sermon pitch as he said, "Faith is an emotional truth. Its value to us is not whether what is accepted on faith can be validated by scientific method. Rather it is the way it affects the person who accepts it. If it makes them feel better, if it gives them hope, helps them to dig out of some tragedy in their life, if it motivates them to be a better person, helps them get through another day, it is potent and true; good medicine for the soul. For me, that's the only way to evaluate something we take on faith." He raised his left hand, "There's science," then raised his right hand, "and there's faith." With that, he smiled magnanimously, nodded a couple of times, then the screen shifted to a car commercial, which was given equal time.

# THIRTY-SEVEN

# A Song of Songs

"I'm wiped up," I said, sprawling back into the downy cushions of Estelle's floral sofa.

"You mean wiped out."

"Isn't that what I said?"

"No."

"What a rich language."

It was about eight at night. I had a brandy sniffer in my hand, or is it snifter? This was rare but I needed relief from the emotion of the day. We had just finished some leftover casserole, something with sausage and beans, that she had gotten out of a Julia Childs cookbook. We were a little light-headed from half a bottle of a "great" Napa Valley cabernet, so she said—what do I know? My sojourn in California had not exposed me to the vineyards. Where I was, they only grew golf courses.

"Mendel, you could use a vacation." Estelle was sitting beside me, comfy in her silk kimono, her legs crossed, a pale calf dangling over her knee.

"You're telling me. Tell the Synagogue Board. I need a sabbatical."

"You haven't been away since that trip to California, right?"

"Right."

"Do you ever hear from that woman that you met?"

"Sarah?" Mention of her name sent a little ripple of excitement through my tired veins.

"Was that her name?"

"Yes."

"Does she write to you?"

"She sent me an invitation to her wedding a few years back."

"Oh?" She took a sip of brandy. The glass was dangling in her hand. "Were you in love with her? We never really talked about it."

"I thought I was at the time. I guess so. Sure."

"Sorry you didn't follow through?"

"No. What is this, the third degree?"

She swirled the cognac and watched it settle. The elbow of her free hand was denting the soft arm of the sofa and she was leaning her head on her hand. "I just wondered. I'm sorry I called you a eunuch the other day."

"Listen, I've been called worse."

"Who by?"

"Nazis."

She choked and gasped with laughter.

"Did you sleep with her?" she finally asked when she had recovered her voice.

I felt my cheeks get red. She was like a teenager. Too many movies. Estelle would never have talked that way ten years ago.

"What about you? Have you slept with anybody since Sam died?"

"I asked you first."

"Yes! I slept with her and I enjoyed it and so did she. Any more questions? Did I wear a condom? No."

"My oh my."

"And she's not the only one. There's a widow in McKeesport who shall remain nameless. So there. Shall I fill out an application? Get references maybe? Satisfied customers? Give a guarantee, money back if not..." I began to laugh, and she joined me then we both fell into one of those uncontrollable fits of laughter that give you the hiccups.

"Listen Estelle, tell me, why all these questions?"

"It's just that I've been thinking about what you said. And..." She put the glass down and took my hand. She looked at me with such tenderness and said, "I just want you to know that I love you."

"You do?" I thought I would have a heart attack.

"Are you alright?" She looked concerned.

"Never felt better in my life. But tell me, how long has this been going on?"

"I don't know. You grow on people, Mendel."

"Like a wart?"

"I'm being serious. Don't make a joke of it." She shook her head and looked at me. "Make a joke; it's one of your endearing qualities—your sad, sweet laughter."

"Now I can't think of anything funny. Only this. I love you too. More than as a sister or a friend. If I could recite the Song of Songs I would."

"Mendel, you are a song enough." She leaned toward me and we kissed, not like we ever had before.

I didn't go back to my apartment at the synagogue that night. In fact she took me upstairs to show me something. It was her bedroom: new teal blue carpet, new curtains, a new bedspread, "in complementary shades."

"Even a new mattress," she said. "The box spring is still good."

We made love. We made love. And I couldn't smell Sam's cigars.

Two months later we were married. Nudelman was the best man. Rabbi Bing did the honors. He was back to his old self, but he was sincere when he said that this was a marriage... What did he say? It makes no difference.

## EPILOGUE

# Deus Ex Machina

A few months later, after I had moved all of my books and clothes into Estelle's house—we had converted the spare bedroom into a library with floor-to-ceiling bookshelves on all four walls—I pulled a pair of pants off of a hanger and put them on. I reached into the pocket and felt a piece of paper. What was it, a receipt for gasoline or a book? I pulled it out, opened it and found Lev's last note. I had forgotten about it.

I read it again, read it several times in fact. I am not a scholar of the New Testament, far from it, but for a Jew I knew a little about the life and death of Yoshua Ben Yosef of Nazareth. Some of the words in the note echoed with words attributed to him. Was Lev saying that he believed himself to be the Messiah? It wasn't possible. He wouldn't have meant that. And yet he had never discouraged the belief, claiming that faith might help people find hope in their lives—a kind of spiritual walker for the psychologically disabled.

If there was any consistency in his conduct that year it was his self-sacrifice and his compassion for the unfortunate, whoever they were. I decided to write about him, not as Morley had or might, and not because I believed him to be the Messiah, rather because I didn't.

Of course, Lev's coming didn't bring on the millennium. His reaching out to the Palestinians didn't end the conflict between Israeli and Palestinian; his giving to the homeless didn't end that problem. His example won't put an end to hatred and mistrust among people, not even in a thousand years, any more than Jesus's teachings have.

It is not useful to think that any single event or the influence of any person will make that kind of difference. What he did do, what we are all capable of, are many small steps in the life-serving direction. To that end, we all carry in us the potential to be a messiah and we should not wait for it to happen. To paraphrase an old Jewish saying: If not now, when; if not me, who?

Our small steps won't stop all the senseless murders, the drug takers, and the drug dealers. They won't stop the child abusers. But when the scale weighs the good against the bad, at least the balance will tip toward life. Well, you've probably heard all that before. No harm in saying it again.

What about the school? Was it buried with Miss Leventhal and the spirit of Lev? No. It went on. The judge made a final decision, letting it continue in the building but giving the trust fund back to the Mossberg family. No, they couldn't use the money to build another shopping center. It still had to be used to benefit the elderly.

In the end their Pittsburgh lawyer convinced the Mossbergs to let the school have one-third of the income. He was persuaded by Selma, Maimonides, and the other old folks, who went to see him in Pittsburgh to tell him how they'd been recommitted to life because of the school.

But there was still a cash shortfall not met by tuition and other contributions. Which brings me to Sam Yanow. You may remember Sam as the wealthy Boltonite who withdrew from the world for a time after his wife died? Most of Lev's year, Sam had been away, an extended trip to Europe. He had rented an apartment in London and gone on trips a week at a time.

He was working on his own private project—identifying Jewish school and synagogue sites, family homes of well-known Jewish scholars or musicians, even businesses, in little towns and villages in Germany and France. If the place hadn't already been marked, Sam would pay for a plaque in German, French, Hebrew, and English. He told me that he had arranged for 37 such plaques that year and hoped to complete another 16. Not bad for one old geezer.

Sam came back home the week Estelle and I were married. We invited him to the little party given by Nudelman and Sarah, but he begged off. Jet lag.

I won't beat around the bush. Sam liked the school, liked what it stood for, and eventually decided to endow it in a big way. That summer we got a new director—Sylvia Lash, a real professional from New York—and a lot of new students, as well. Schweig was the only teacher who didn't stay on. It was mutual.

Selma is still running the office and baking her tea cakes. Maimonides is actually teaching a course in Jewish mysticism and helping with the garden. The school is now planting an orchard and hopes to market organically grown preserves, using Selma's grandmother's recipes. Imagine that! Selma still had them, so she led us to believe. She made some plum jam and the kids couldn't get enough of it. She puts— There I go again.

It's all going as Lev planned it. We are now raising funds to build a permanent residence for the homeless to get them out of tents and the loft of the barn in winter. If you'd like to help out, a check would be welcome. So far, 18 homeless men and women have gotten skill training—in the kitchen, working with the cows and chickens, or cultivating the garden. All but two have found jobs. Izzy Bortz runs a placement service, no charge to the employer.

The first graduation ceremony for the homeless was another one of those tear-evoking events. We are thinking of seeking an endowment from Scott Paper Company for our contribution to Kleenex sales. (Estelle says I should take that out. She's looking over my shoulder. But I don't think so.) After all, tears and laughter go together in life.

So things are going fine. The only big dispute the Board has this year is what to call the school. Some want to name it after Lev. Some don't. Some want to name it after Miss Leventhal. Some don't. What do you think?

www.ingramcontent.com/pod-product-compliance
Lightning Source LLC
Chambersburg PA
CBHW020419110726
47899CB00006B/2058